ACPL, Laramie, WY   8/2016
000400947156
O'Rourke, Frank,
Ellen and the barber : three love stories o
Pieces: 1

in honor of
• *Kathy Krafczik* •
presented by the
Friends of the Library

D0021289

Ellen and the Barber

PREVIOUS TITLES BY FRANK O'ROURKE

Burton and Stanley
The Abduction of Virginia Lee
The Swift Runner
A Mule for the Marquesa
Instant Gold
A Private Anger and Flight and Pursuit
The Affair of the Bumbling Briton
The Affair of the Blue Pig
The Affair of John Donne
The Affair of Chief Strongheart
The Affair of Jolie Madame
The Affair of Swan Lake
The Affair of the Red Mosaic
The Bright Morning
The Springtime Fancy
Window in the Dark
The Bride Stealer
The Far Mountains
The Last Ride
The Diamond Hitch

MAJOR FILMS FROM THE FOLLOWING NOVELS

The Bravados
The Professionals (from A Mule for the Marquesa)
The Great Bank Robbery

Ellen and the Barber

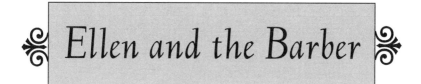

THREE LOVE STORIES
OF THE THIRTIES

Frank O'Rourke

ST. MARTIN'S PRESS ❧ NEW YORK

ALBANY COUNTY
PUBLIC LIBRARY
LARAMIE, WYOMING

THOMAS DUNNE BOOKS.
An imprint of St. Martin's Press.

ELLEN AND THE BARBER. Copyright © 1998 by Edith Carlson O'Rourke. All rights reserved. Printed in the United States of America. No part of this book may be used or reproduced in any manner whatsoever without written permission except in the case of brief quotations embodied in critical articles or reviews. For information, address St. Martin's Press, 175 Fifth Avenue, New York, N.Y. 10010.

Design by Ellen R. Sasahara

Library of Congress Cataloging-in-Publication Data

O'Rourke, Frank.
    Ellen and the barber : three love stories of the thirties / Frank O'Rourke.—1st ed.
       p.   cm.
    "Thomas Dunne books."
    Contents: Ellen and the barber—Miriam—Vera.
    ISBN 0-312-19263-0
    1. Man-woman relationships—United States—Fiction.
2. Depressions—United States—Fiction.   3. Nineteen thirties—Fiction.   4. Love stories, American.   I. Title.
PS3529.R58E45   1998
813'.54—dc21   98-18715
                                             CIP

First Edition: September 1998

10 9 8 7 6 5 4 3 2 1

To the editor,
Ruth Cavin

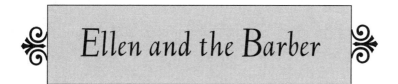

Ellen and the Barber

One

T HE OLD BARBER had been threatening to quit for three years, and that spring of 1928 he made it stick. He wrote the state secretary of the Barbers' Association to find a new man for Cherrygrove, and began packing preparatory to joining his daughter and son-in-law in California. The new barber visited town the day before the old barber left, agreed on arrangements, and rented the vacant bungalow that was next door to the depot agent's house. The new barber moved in over the weekend with his wife and two-year-old son. His name was Jack Bascombe. He was a good-looking young man of twenty-seven who seemed devoted to his family. He lacked the shaving touch that came from long experience, but he was a better scissors man than his predecessor, and children climbed his chair onto the seat-board without argument.

The barbershop was located in the right front corner of the drugstore, and between customers Bascombe got into the habit of sitting at the soda fountain for a cigaret and some chitchat with the druggist, who had been postmaster from 1913 until 1921, at which time the Republican spoils system worked downward through the Democratic echelons and removed his sinecure. When the new postmaster moved the office across the street, the druggist rented the empty corner to the old barber and tried to make a living selling patent medicines and sodas, but the odds were against him.

In 1922 the druggist shook hands on a deal with McGonigle, the local bootlegger, and remodeled the stockroom behind the soda fountain. McGonigle stored and sold grain alcohol to customers, who continued out the rear door into the backyard to spike their near beer and get as drunk as they pleased. The druggist prospered moderately, but the spring Bascombe came to town was the time his wife laid down the law. Their daughter was a skinny girl with buck teeth, red hair, and a nasty disposition honed daily by the impossibility of forgetting her given name. In a strange fit of misplaced Grecian spelling, her parents had christened her Menauklis, and the name had become an incubus to the child. The druggist's wife told him it was time to take their daughter elsewhere, change her name, and give them all a fresh start.

The druggist offered the store to Bascombe, and Jack knew that it could make a good living for a barber willing to hire a clerk to sell sodas and sundries while he managed the bootlegging between haircuts, but he didn't have the money. Bascombe made an arrangement with the bootlegger. McGonigle bought the drugstore and rented it to Bascombe. Bascombe hired the youngest Gochman girl to clerk and jerk sodas; then he and McGonigle built three hidden panels into the back wall of the stockroom, and screwed clothes hooks into the outer sheathing between the studs. They kept the pint and half-pint bottles of grain alcohol in socks suspended from the hooks on chalklines. Bascombe could open a hidden panel, pull up a sock, sell a bottle, and be back shaving his customer before the sock stopped swaying. To celebrate his prosperity, Bascombe took his wife to the first spring dance in the new pavilion.

They made a fine couple on the floor. Bascombe knew nearly everybody by that time, and his wife was so good-natured it was hard not to like her. She danced with other men, and Bascombe danced with their wives. He was leading Mrs. Busker through a waltz when a face whirled slowly past, the eyes met his, the head revolved, the eyes met his again, and vanished into the crowd.

Bascombe remarked to Mrs. Busker that he was beginning to know everybody, but there were still a few strangers. He pointed them out and Mrs. Busker named them, and somewhere in the middle of the bunch he nodded casually toward the girl whose eyes had met his. Mrs. Busker said it wasn't surprising he hadn't met Ellen Kellner because she was a senior at Bent Fork High School and stayed with her sister Twila who worked in Bent Fork. Bascombe nodded pleasantly and danced on. He still remembered Ellen Kellner's face when April blended into May.

ELLEN KELLNER WAS an extremely pretty girl. She had long, dark brown hair and a lovely slim body, and huge, slightly protruding brown eyes that seemed continually straining to reach for, and absorb, all the life around her. Few people recognized that look. It was the look of a girl frantic to become a woman before she had dreamed through all the priceless tales of childhood, all the stories of imagination that bridged many an impossible torrent in later, crueler years when dreams dissolved into the reality of life.

In the spring Ellen Kellner's fancy lightly turned to thoughts of men. She thought of men in other seasons too, but spring brought forth new dreams that kept her in front of the mirror, studying the face and body that intrigued her. Her sister often said, "Kid, where *did* you get it?" in loving admiration of Ellen's triumph over heredity. Their father had been an ordinary-looking man, and while their mother was certainly a good-looking woman, there were no precedents for Ellen.

She finished the tenth grade in 1926, and to no one's surprise chose to complete her high school education in Bent Fork. Living with her sister was thriftier than boarding in Burnside, the other nearby town with a four-year high school. Ellen studied hard and adopted a retiring attitude that got her through the difficult opening weeks in a strange school. At the end of the first semester she had earned a B-plus average, and her teachers were pleased with her conduct and clean-scrubbed look in a time of bobbed hair, too much makeup, and worsening manners. Ellen wore her hair long and her face bare, and caught the eye of every boy in school. The girls watched her with suspicious envy until they realized that she was making no effort to steal their beaus; toward the end of her junior year she was elected to the Tuning Forks, Bent Fork High School's most exclusive club.

Ellen spent the summer at home, sewing new clothes for her senior year. Her mother was an expert seamstress who had made all her daughters' clothes until they learned to sew. Twila's first big purchase, upon going to work in Bent Fork, was a Singer. It was surprising how a wardrobe grew at small cost, starting with yard goods, thread, buttons, and patterns. Ellen's excitement was heightened when her mother let her attend the first spring dance at the new pavilion built the summer before. She had a fine time, obeyed Twila's stern dictum not to flirt, and saw one interesting man who turned out to be the new barber.

Her senior year was a quiet triumph. Her grades held at B-plus and she was one of the cheerleaders in the frenetic line that led the student body during football and basketball games. She attended several movies and two school dances with boys who treated her with awed respect. Her last semester was a time of happy relaxation; with more than enough credits to graduate, she jumped at the chance to take two easy electives. One was Senior Civics, a class in patriotic responsibility taught by the athletic coach, who led his students on a comfortable tour through the ascending levels of American government. He was an excellent teacher, just as he was a good coach, only twenty-nine years old and, according to the critics, destined for a great career.

A bachelor, he treated all high school girls with the same manly kindness and courtesy, so that his last-period class never failed to be stimulating. Often, as the semester drew to a close, he walked from the classroom with several girls and a like number of boys, usually lettermen, and answered questions until they were nipped by the bell. He waved goodbye at the west stairwell and ran downstairs to his office at the south end of the gym, where assistant coaches, players, and the janitor lounged on the swaybacked couch and rickety chairs while replaying their male victories and defeats.

Four years before, teaching and coaching in a town smaller than Cherrygrove, the coach had taken a squad of seven farm boys to the state basketball tournament and won the championship. The Bent Fork alumni wasted no time persuading him to change his address, nor had he disappointed them. In his short tenure he had won two conference football titles and taken his basketball team to three quarter-finals in the state tournament; and yet, his greatest talent was not coaching young men.

His avocation, from the time he could tell the difference between pants and petticoats, was seduction. He was in clover at the state university; by the time he graduated and began his career in, of all places, his own hometown, he had become a farmbelt artist in the seduction of young women. Nor did he deal in wholesale lots; only the prettiest, most shapely, most likely virginal became his targets. During the three-year stay in his hometown, he exercised iron self-discipline and the old-fashioned belief that molesting a hometown girl was akin to rape, and honed his artistry in distant communities. When his big chance came, as he knew it must, he took up residence in Bent Fork with absolute confidence of victory on all playing fields.

The coach adhered to a strict routine: At the beginning of each school year he chose a girl from the senior class to become the recipient of his attentions. She must be eighteen before graduation, and unaware of his interest until the final week of the school year. It might seem that the coach placed insurmountable handicaps in his own path, but he knew a great deal about eighteen-year-old women. He was a tall, broad-shouldered man with jet-black hair, dark brown eyes, and craggy features that strongly resembled Red Grange, and he made no effort to conceal the natural attraction he had for women. He treated it as a jockey-strap itch over which he had no control, and maintained his steadfast courtesy in and out of school. He noticed Ellen Kellner during her junior year, and unhesitantly picked her as the class of 1928's offering on his altar.

She excited him as no other girl had, with her combination of natural beauty and big-eyed guilelessness. She seemed to be genuinely innocent of her effect on boys; even more astonishing was the fact that other girls liked her. The coach approached the last week of school with mounting anticipation. If all went as planned, he should perform the rite on the day after graduation, when Ellen was no longer under the quasi-legal aegis of the school system.

Ellen was the belle of the senior prom. She came with her date, the graduating fullback, and danced every set—with him, with other boys, several teachers, and finally the coach, who led her through a sedate waltz at arm's length, the perfect picture of the good teacher who cared about his pupils right to the end of their school days. He asked what she planned to do after graduation, and when she admitted giving her future very little thought, he expressed the hope she would attend college. Ellen told him that she couldn't afford it. He nodded understandingly and inquired if she intended to stay in Bent Fork after graduation, and she replied that her sister and mother were going to Omaha the morning after the ceremonies to visit her older brother, so she would stay in the apartment until their return the following Monday.

The coach danced a minute in harmonious silence, smiling in his teacherish way, before asking if she would like to celebrate her freedom by having a malted milk with him, not as a teacher, but as an old friend who wanted to see her off on the right foot in the cold, cruel world. Ellen was so surprised, and flattered, that she demurely nodded and asked what time he would call. Around eight, he told her.

Ellen lay awake at least ten minutes that night, wondering why the coach had noticed her. The next day was a steady rush of preparation for the graduation ceremonies that evening, readying her dress and doing her hair; and that night she marched into the auditorium with her class, sat through the speeches, rose and filed up the left-hand steps, crossed the stage, received her diploma and ceremonial handshakes, and went down the right-hand side a graduated woman. The next morning she saw her mother and sister off for Omaha, and passed the day in a state of euphoria, wondering where the coach would take her. She had other, more unsettling thoughts vaguely connected with his virility, but that was mooning. The coach was so much older that he could not possibly entertain such ideas. How could he, a grown man with a reputation that defied gossip, which meant it must be secretly wicked! When she answered the doorbell at eight-fifteen, he stood holding one red rose in a blue tissue-paper funnel, smiling at her radiant beauty.

Had her family gotten off safely for Omaha? Good. He took her arm and escorted her out to his car parked on the dark side street. He handed her into the 1928 Model A Ford two-door, went around and got behind the wheel, started the engine, and spoke above the clatter "—you like homemade ice cream?" and when Ellen said she loved it, he laughed happily and told her that a friend had invited them out to his river cabin to help eat up a two-quart freezerful, and if that wasn't better than a malted milk, he'd eat his hat, and if she was still game after that, they'd all go dancing at Clancy's. Clancy's was a roadhouse seven miles south of Bent Fork on the Jefferson highway, a place that high school students heard about and never entered.

The coach drove around the block and turned west on Bent Fork Avenue in the cool May night. He drove five miles west, turned south on a country road, and west again on a lane parallel to the Buckhorn River into the clearing behind the cabin. The cabin was dark. "Darn it, where are they?" he said. "Well, let's go in and take a look at the freezer." They did, and after the coach lit a Coleman, they found the ice cream frozen stiff. He pulled the dasher and told Ellen to lick it while he rustled up the eating equipment. He filled their dishes and led her out on the front porch, where they ate to their heart's content and watched the shimmer of moon and starlight on the river. The coach was wearing a short-sleeved polo shirt with a pair of white seersucker pants and perforated white sports oxfords. He looked cool and manly eating his ice cream, using his spoon to point out interesting things along the river, and telling her a story she had never heard before—the battle between the early settlers and the Indians, fought less than two miles from where they sat.

"How about another dish?"

Ellen refused politely. They went back inside and the coach rinsed the dishes and stacked them on the drainboard. He was a pleasure to watch, a man with deft, sure movements, his eyes shining with the joy of living.

He wound up the phonograph, put on a record, and tripped the catch. He extended his arms, Ellen stepped into them, and they danced around the cabin to the tune of "Sleepy Time Gal," and it was better than the senior prom because he held her closer and she felt his face against her hair. The record ended and he said, "Like it?" and when she nodded, kept one arm around her waist while he rewound the machine and put on another record.

Ellen lost track of time. They danced, changed records, and danced again, until she wondered where his friends were, because the ice cream would melt before they arrived. Deep inside, she knew they were not coming. Then, at some indefinite moment, she began to feel him generally and specifically, and found herself dancing so close they barely had space to move their feet. She responded eagerly when he kissed her, and before the kiss ended they were in the bedroom, her clothes had vanished, and his too, and she knew she should stop, but curiosity and desire were too strong for common sense, and in no time at all she joined the ranks of the women of the world, or at least that was how Fannie Hurst and other writers expressed the loss of virginity in ladylike words. It hurt, there was little real enjoyment, and she certainly did not learn much, but the second time was better, and before they drove home at five A.M. she felt as if she had been making love for years.

Two

I NSTEAD OF GOING about his summer business as chief counselor at a boys' camp in the Rocky Mountains northwest of Denver, the coach wired his resignation and stayed in Bent Fork. Since Ellen was now a graduate, there was no need for secrecy if certain rules of conduct were observed. The coach called for Ellen early in the evening and brought her home by midnight at the latest; between the proper covers of that etiquette book were the pages written two and three times a week in the river cabin. Ellen soon learned that the cabin was owned by the coach's best friend, a bachelor lawyer, but that safeguard was no reason for complacency. And one morning at breakfast, her sister spoke without warning.

"Are you taking precautions?"

Ellen was so shocked she could not speak for a moment. How could Twila know? Was that old saying really true? Did it show on a girl's face after she had relations with a man?

"Well?"

Ellen found her voice. "Yes."

"Where did you learn?"

"He showed me."

"He would!"

"Twila, can you see it in my face?"

"No," Twila said, and had to smile. "That's a lot of bunk!"

"But how *do* they tell?"

"Usually by the size of your stomach," Twila said, and that was the last time she mentioned it. "Now get going, see if you can find a job today."

Ellen looked dutifully for work, that day and many others, and soon faced the unpalatable truth that jobs were available in the canning factory, in the stores, and in the cafés. She could attend beauty school and learn how to give permanent waves and manicure nails, but a job with a future? The coach did his best to find something worthwhile, and the lawyer was moved by his friend's passion to look even further, but their efforts were fruitless. The lawyer told the coach to persuade Ellen to start business college as soon as possible, where she could learn typing, shorthand, and bookkeeping, all the tools needed by a stenographer in one of the offices that were forever losing girls and hiring new ones for reasons as numerous as the girls themselves.

"Can you afford the tuition?" the coach asked, the night he made the suggestion.

Ellen nodded. Twila had agreed to pay the tuition out of savings if Ellen would start with the class that convened on July fifth and graduated the week before Christmas. The coach urged her to enroll on the last night in June, and the following morning Ellen enrolled at the Bent Fork College of Business and began classes on July fifth. She recognized a dozen former classmates and knew that competition for future jobs would be fierce, come Christmastime. She told the coach that night that she was not at all sure of getting a decent job. The coach patted her bare behind and reassured her. Ellen rolled over and reassured him.

AS THE NEW school year began its arc through time, Ellen Kellner met her competition head-on and lost the fight without laying a glove on her opponent. How could a woman defeat the game of football? All the coach's energy was focused on the dirty-clean smell of sweat and rubbing alcohol and leather, the sight and sound and palm-tingling feel of blocking, tackling, punting, sin-

gle wing to the right, right guard pulling, quarterback barking sig-
nals in a voice that went falsetto under the strain of momentous
decision as the ball was snapped and the boys ran formations on
the browning grass in the crisp fall sunshine . . . where thoughts
of carnal love were erased from the coach's mind.

If he had not exercised his self-discipline, the coach would
have come under the scrutiny of the school board for dating a former pupil eleven years his junior and certainly not the proper wife
for a coach as good as he was. He did not keep one final tryst and
murmur foolish words in an effort to ease the pain of parting. He
had too much common sense and kindness to needlessly hurt anyone, particularly a girl as loving as Ellen. It was better to disappear
behind a football and let time blur the memory; it ended the first
day he walked out on the practice field and blew one sharp, sweet
blast on the silver whistle dangling around his neck. Ellen Kellner
receded into yesterday and joined the gallery of faces once held
dear.

For her part, Ellen at first refused to accept the truth. She began
going home on weekends, where her mother praised her hard work
and reminded her how practical it was to get a good job and share
apartment expenses with Twila. Her mother said, "Write some
shorthand for me, dear," and Ellen made a lot of chicken tracks in
her steno notebook and listened to the silent sound of her breaking heart. But a heart can break for just so long, and Ellen was too
sensible not to eventually understand that her affair had no
chance of surviving the coach's love for his work. As the fall wore
on, and the football team began what was destined to become a
record-breaking winning streak, Ellen gradually appreciated what
the coach had meant the night he talked about his work.

He had, he said, no illusions about the earth-shaking importance of coaching, but he knew, as all good coaches knew, that the
sweat and pain and work did more than win games. He knew that
it could, and sometimes did, help a boy wrestle with himself at
some later date, and give him the courage and discipline to make
a big decision that would help win a truly important game in the
big bowl of life. At which time the coach always told himself,

"Bullshit!" and went about the enjoyable task of picking the right girl for his next rite of spring.

ELLEN KELLNER WAS sick of hearing the business college teachers say that it wasn't the shape of the good stenographer that counted, but the size of the brain that kept her ears apart. Ellen knew she was the best all-around student in the class. Her shorthand was fast and accurate, her typing was the cleanest, and bookkeeping was easy. Twila was always available to show her how school methods were changed for practical use in real offices. Ellen knew she would graduate with an excellent recommendation, but getting a good job was another story. Twila said that a lot of things seemed to be going wrong in business, had been heading in that direction for over a year. Twila could not put her finger on the trouble, but she told Ellen that her boss had done about ten percent less business than in 1927. Whether that figure had general meaning, or was just the reflection of one particular business, Twila did not know, but she warned Ellen to find a job in some good, solid business, no matter if it paid less than more attractive offers, and then stick to it until she nailed her spot down.

Ellen saw the coach twice that fall. The first time was during Homecoming Parade the day before Thanksgiving and brought back a rush of emotions that she had thought firmly buried. She was walking downtown when the parade came up Bent Fork Avenue from the river bridge; she saw the coach on a big flatbed truck with his football team, waving to the crowds on both sidewalks. He did not see her, or made no sign if he did, and was out of sight in a minute. The second occasion came when Twila's regular friend, a traveling man from Omaha, was in town on his monthly swing and invited Ellen to dine with them at Clancy's. They had a right front corner table with a good view of the dining room, and were just finishing their dessert when the coach came in with his lawyer friend and two married couples, the husbands members of the school board, a fact that made the coach's presence in the roadhouse legitimate. Twila managed to get Ellen into the powder room before the coach was seated, and from that point it was easy to walk directly to the car, forestalling any accidental meeting.

Ellen graduated from business college on schedule, and while she waited for the Christmas vacation period to pass so she could start looking for work, she decorated the apartment, shopped for presents, and took the Friday afternoon train home. She piled her purchases in a window seat and took the aisle, and someone said, "Hello, Miss Kellner," and she looked up at a man about the coach's age standing in the aisle with his arms full of packages, a brown fedora clinging precariously to the back of his head where it must have been jostled by the crowd boarding the train. He said, "I'm Jack Bascombe," and went on to say that he was the new barber in Cherrygrove, or maybe not the new barber anymore, but just the barber. "We've never been introduced, but I saw you at the opening dance in the pavilion last spring."

"Sit down, Mr. Bascombe," Ellen said politely. "Rest your arms."

"Thanks"—Bascombe threw the front seat forward. *"Phew!* Been Christmas shopping for the wife and boy, the boy's that age where in three days he can break a toy guaranteed for a year." Bascombe laughed, a good laugh with his head thrown back and his white teeth gleaming. He piled his packages on the window seat and sat facing her, and talked about the usual things newly met people used to fill in the duration of a short train ride. When they pulled into Cherrygrove he helped her with her packages, tipped his hat, followed her through the vestibule down the steps onto the platform in the cold late afternoon dusk, and went his own way with a brisk, light-footed walk.

It was nice to see a man shopping for his wife and child, and not only that, a man who knew small towns well enough not to walk with her from the station and cause talk; and yet . . . Rubbing her nose with a cold mitten, Ellen started home. It had to be her imagination. No married man with a child would look at her the way Bascombe had looked, or the way she thought he had looked. Not disrespectfully, or leering, but an interested look, as if they were both unattached and ought to explore the possibilities. And then she thought, with a shiver, was it herself doing the looking?

IMMEDIATELY AFTER THE Christmas holidays, Ellen Kellner presented herself to Mrs. Rosenzweig in the office of Rosenzweig's Dress Shop on the north side of Bent Fork Avenue between Fourth and Fifth Streets. She answered Mrs. Rosenzweig's questions to the best of her ability, demonstrated her skills, and was offered the job at a starting salary of $12.50 a week, six days a week from eight to six with an hour off for lunch, one week's paid vacation per year, and no fraternizing with the customers.

Ellen kept the books, took dictation, typed, got the morning and afternoon mail from the Rosenzweigs' post office box, and found herself enjoying the work. Mr. Rosenzweig was a quiet, kindly man who treated her with the nicest manners she had ever known. He was not a chaser, and he tended strictly to the backroom alteration and repair work, while Mrs. Rosenzweig waited on trade with the help of one saleslady, a married woman in her forties, mother of two children, precisely the size to wear the dresses sold to more matronly women of her generation. Mrs. Rosenzweig could sell spit to a camel, was scrupulously honest, and had an eagle eye for putting the right dress on the right customer. Ellen was delighted to learn that her mother's three measurements for a perfect-fitting dress were Mrs. Rosenzweig's sacred guidelines: the actual bust size, which meant running the tape measure across the shoulder blades in back and around, the actual waist size, and measuring over the largest part of the hips.

"Ladies cheat," Mrs. Rosenzweig said. "Not me—themselves!"

Those ladies were the wives and grown-up daughters of businessmen, doctors, lawyers, and anyone else who belonged to the loosely defined upper middle-class in towns the size of Bent Fork. Mrs. Rosenzweig had captured eighty percent of that clientele whose exclusive membership was almost entirely determined by money. The Rosenzweigs went east twice a year to buy clothes, dressed their own shop windows with artful simplicity, wrote their own ads, and sold dresses other stores did not, or could not, acquire. They were the first Jewish people Ellen had ever met, much less known, and after three months she could not understand why so many people—including her own mother and sister—spoke so disparagingly of Jews. Was it a Midwest prejudice that was born into small-town people?

Ellen slowly learned the business; by spring, she was learning more and more about the town, how the moneyed people of Bent Fork spent their money, where they spent it, and what they did with the articles they bought. She made the astonishing discovery that Mrs. Rosenzweig and the saleslady were not only in the business of selling, but of necessity experts in diplomacy and professional secrecy. Who would guess that in a town of ten thousand, certain well-to-do men kept mistresses? Ellen watched those women shop, made the charge entries, and mailed the statements to addresses identified only by post office box numbers. One day, getting the afternoon mail, she saw a well-known businessman open one of those boxes, and in a delayed flash of insight that had taken three months, knew which very handsome woman was wearing a fifty-dollar dress for the benefit of which married man.

One day in May, Mrs. Rosenzweig took Ellen into the fitting room, had her put on one of the spring frocks, and walk back and forth in front of the triple mirror. She arranged Ellen in a simple, unstrained pose and circled her, eyes narrowed, mouth puckered up as if it was holding her habitual row of common pins. Ellen kicked off her shoes and slipped into the high-heeled pumps Mrs. Rosenzweig took from a shoe box. The heels increased her height at least three inches, and the frock and pumps fit her perfectly, more proof of Mrs. Rosenzweig's eye for sizes.

"When it gets a little warmer," Mrs. Rosenzweig said, "I want you to wear a dress when I tell you to. Have you got a friend?"

"A friend?"

"Gentleman friend!" Mrs. Rosenzweig said impatiently. "What else?"

"Oh—no, Mrs. Rosenzweig."

"You have no friend? I don't believe it."

Ellen started to explain, but Mrs. Rosenzweig seemed to understand. "Makes no difference, you wear the dresses when I say so, it's good for business."

Three

B Y SPRING, DESPITE his wife's foreboding that bootlegging would strip away their decency and smite them down, Bascombe had never felt better. Barbering earned him a decent living, the drugstore was breaking even, and the barber had discovered how much easy money there was in the world. He put his bootlegging profits into a safe deposit box in the Bent Fork First National Bank; by the end of May he had sixteen hundred dollars in the box, with no end in sight. His wife could not deny that he was doing a job people demanded, and besides, she liked a drink now and then as well as he did; but still, in the midst of growing wealth, she began looking at their son, then at Jack, in meaningful conclusions silently drawn. Bascombe gave her all the money she wanted and went on about his business.

On a late morning in May, coming from the bank, he saw Ellen Kellner for the first time since meeting her on the train the Saturday before Christmas. She was entering Rosenzweig's Dress Shop on the other side of Bent Fork Avenue; Bascombe stalled a few minutes, fiddling with the spark and gas levers, pumping the clutch and brake pedals as if something were wrong, but she did not emerge. Bascombe backed out and drove for home, and during the week learned that Ellen worked at Rosenzweig's, the best ladies' shop in Bent Fork. Bascombe had thought of her several times during the winter; it was damned foolishness, but he could not get her out of his mind. In a way, it was not entirely his fault.

Bascombe, like the coach, was one of those unfortunate men who attracted women. He had discovered that strange fact soon after he reached a youthful stage in life, and spent two more years trying to unravel the mystery of whatever it was that made girls pay him the most blatant compliments. When he understood the secret, and accomplished the fact, in act, he enjoyed it so much that he marveled at his previous ignorance. Nor had age brought contempt for doing what Bascombe felt was the best thing in life. Bascombe was an oddity. He was not a promiscuous man, but wherever he went, no matter how he resisted, it was only a matter of time before some woman dragged him into bed.

Marriage had not changed his situation. He loved his wife, doted on their son, but at irregular intervals women appeared. Bascombe had developed a fine degree of selectivity, and sufficient self-discipline, to shrug off or ignore most of the overtures. He tried to pick the most worthy women, but he was acutely aware that he could not choose the best until he sampled the wares. Women as beautiful as Ellen Kellner were scarce as hens' teeth in Bascombe's world. He might miss the very best if he did not have her.

He was not a conniver. Once his mind was made up, he moved with direct simplicity, but he might have gone on wanting Ellen Kellner for years if Dave McGonigle had not come down with a bad case of influenza. McGonigle did not trust his brother Charlie to take delivery of grain alcohol from the supplier who came down from the Missouri River country at prearranged times and transfer the five-gallon cans from his truck to McGonigle's Dodge coupe. McGonigle sent Jack Bascombe to the selected spot on the Buckhorn River six miles west of Bent Fork. Bascombe made payment and brought the load back to the McGonigle farm without incident. When the doctor gave McGonigle strict orders to take it easy the rest of the year, Bascombe assumed the additional duties. He told his wife that he would be doing a good deal of night driving, but not to worry, there was no danger and a lot more profit, because McGonigle had to cut him in on a bigger slice of the melon.

Toward the end of August, Bascombe was so familiar with pickup details that he had memorized the topography of the Buckhorn River from a sandpit eight miles southeast of Bent Fork to a row of summer cabins six miles west. The supplier lived somewhere in the Dakotas and sent a letter addressed to the post office box McGonigle rented in Bent Fork. Bascombe visited the post office twice a week, read the letter—if delivered—giving place, time, and date, and drove out to McGonigle's farm to get the cash. He met the supplier on the stated date, and brought the alcohol straight back to the farm where Charlie stored the five-gallon cans in the hideout. Thus, on the last Monday in August, Bascombe closed his barbershop and drove to Bent Fork at four in the afternoon, parked on Lincoln Avenue, and walked around the block into the post office. He took out his key ring, opened the box, and found a letter. Turning, he nearly bumped into Ellen Kellner, who was opening an adjacent box. Bascombe had been trying to evolve a foolproof plan of meeting her; suddenly it was done. He tipped his hat and smiled.

"Hello."

Ellen looked up. "Oh, hello, Mr. Bascombe."

She looked wonderful in her light summer dress, arms bare, hair combed smoothly heavy over her shoulders, face innocent of makeup, the tiny drops of sweat on her upper lip making Bascombe shiver with desire. They were alone in the right-hand hallway of the post office, two strangers unmet in the first moments of their meeting, yet somehow joined together before they closed their boxes and walked toward the front entrance. Bascombe had no idea how she felt, if whatever it was in him was working, but he forgot everything else in the urgency of the moment.

"Miss Kellner?"

"Yes."

"I want to see you again."

She did not look shocked, or say coquettishly, "Why, Mr. Bascombe, and you a married man!" Her reply was equally direct: "Where?"

They stopped walking. Bascombe took out his notebook and mechanical pencil. He wrote the number of the post office box, tore out the sheet, and handed it to her.

"Write me where and when. I look at this box Mondays and Fridays."

People rounded the corner of the hallway. Bascombe tipped his hat and walked away, out the front entrance and around the block to his car, before he realized what they had done. His own boldness was compulsive. Hers was frightening.

Four

T HE STOCK MARKET crash did not concern Ellen Kellner until she heard the Rosenzweigs discussing falling sales and growing unemployment in the east. Even then, she paid little attention to the danger signs. For two months she had felt like a pinboy in a bowling alley, setting up solid racks of reasons for not writing Jack Bascombe, then watching the black ball of her frustration hurtle down the alley and score perfect strikes on morality. She mailed the letter on November first, telling Bascombe that her sister was going to Cherrygrove for the weekend, so she would be waiting on the corner behind the apartment house at eight o'clock Saturday night.

Twila took the afternoon train to visit their mother, who was very proud of her two fine, hardworking daughters who held down such good jobs and lived in their own two-bedroom apartment. Ellen ate an early supper, took a leisurely bath, and dressed; at five minutes of eight she buttoned up her old mackinaw, pulled a stocking cap over her ears, and took the back stairs to the alley behind the garages. She walked out to the street and waited in the shadow of the big elm tree twenty feet from the corner; and a dozen heartbeats later a car swung off Bent Fork Avenue and nosed slowly down the side street. Ellen ran across the wet grass and jumped into the Model A before it stopped rolling. Bascombe released his clutch, circled the block, and headed west on Bent

Fork Avenue. He smelled cleanly of good soap and bay rum, but that was how a barber should smell. Ellen shivered.

"Cold tonight."

"Sure is."

That seemed to exhaust Bascombe's small talk. He drove west five miles, turned south off the highway, and followed a zigzag course into a clearing above the river. He led her around the dark bulk of a cabin, unlocked the front door, and ushered her inside. It was warm from the fire in the big base burner started by someone earlier that evening. Bascombe said, "Wait a minute," and felt his way across the room, scratched a match, and lit the Coleman. Ellen did not know whether to laugh or cry, but Bascombe gave her no time for reflective choice. He took her arm, she took his, and they danced an awkward minuet between familiar pieces of furniture to the bed, undressed, and made love for such a long time that the fire burned low and the room chilled before they had the sense to get under the covers. Once there, it only seemed proper to exchange a few words of newly minted intimacy. Bascombe proved he had the gift of gab.

"Jesus!" he said. "Where have you been all my life?"

It was not a question. It was a blunt affirmation of the answer they had already supplied. With the complicated simplicity of most animals and few humans, all they needed to do was nourish the passion begun in a silence that was likely to continue with a minimum of words for as long as circumstances and desire existed. But every hill and dale in the bed was as familiar to Ellen as her memories of the times she had visited this cabin with the coach. Had he returned? Who shared his homemade ice cream on a soft May night? Discretion held her tongue, but she could not restrain her laughter. She sat up in bed, held the covers under her chin, and laughed until the tears wet her cheeks. Bascombe rubbed her back and said, "What's the joke?"

"I just feel good."

"Me too."

Toward morning Bascombe was seized with a mild spasm of explanation. He told Ellen that McGonigle's lawyer owned the cabin and had given Dave a key long ago in case Dave wanted to hold random meetings with certain parties from the Dakotas. Dave being sick, Bascombe was doing all the legwork, hence his knowledge of the cabin; but it was not winterized. "Do you have any ideas about a warmer place?"

"Not offhand."

"Don't worry about it," Bascombe said. "I'll think of something."

He let her off at the corner behind the apartment house at six A.M. with no excessive expression of emotion. His conduct suited Ellen to a T; she had no silly, sentimental feeling either. She felt whole for the first time in a year, and she faced the truth that she had recognized the solution to her natural need in Bascombe as surely as he saw his own in hers; if they could maintain that spirit of honesty, they would be all right. But, God, how she would love to walk into the lawyer's office and thank him for the continued use of the cabin.

After Christmas, obeying the orders of his doctor, McGonigle retired permanently from bootlegging. Bascombe was busier than ever, taking wholesale deliveries from the Dakota suppliers and keeping his growing circle of customers happy. No one had ever trailed McGonigle to a rendezvous, and Bascombe proved to be more devious and slippery than Dave. But Bascombe did not neglect his barbering. He was always on duty in the morning, ready to cut hair and shave faces. He seemed to thrive on hard work and lack of sleep.

Truth was, he was on the verge of exhaustion by the end of December. After a month of catch-as-catch-can meetings with Ellen, Bascombe solved the problem in daring fashion. On the first Friday after New Year's, he closed the barbershop at three o'clock on a slow afternoon, and drove to Bent Fork. He parked under the big elm tree beside the Kritchfield Apartments, and knocked on the manager's door.

Half an hour later, the manager was congratulating himself on renting one of the expensive main-floor apartments in the west wing to such a nice traveling man who explained that he was gone a good deal of the time covering a territory that extended into Wyoming and Montana, and needed a comfortable place to rest en route to his regional headquarters in Omaha. He arranged for the manager to furnish the apartment with a few essential pieces, the most important a big, soft bed for a man in need of rest. Bascombe's letter to Ellen told her to give the manager a week to furnish the place, then take the enclosed key, go down the west wing stairs from her top-floor apartment, and along the west wing to the last apartment on the west side of the hall, unlock the door and step inside.

By the end of January their system was working splendidly. Whenever Bascombe could get away, he mailed a letter. Whenever Ellen saw free time coming, she mailed a letter. Each tried to accommodate the other; if one, or both failed, there was always a next time. Once they established a rhythm, Ellen excused herself after supper by telling Twila she was going to the library. She actually walked the three blocks to the library, checked out a book, and hurried back to the west wing apartment. She stayed with Bascombe until ten o'clock, the library's closing time, and went upstairs refreshed from an evening of educational reading, courtesy of Andrew Carnegie. By the first of April, Twila remarked that she had never seen Ellen looking better, and the way she was reading books, she'd go through the entire library in a few years.

"What do you like best?"

"History."

"How come?"

"It seems to come easy for me."

Ellen did not explain that the history section was easiest to reach as she entered the library, and never crowded, giving her space to quickly choose a book, check it out, and hurry back to the apartment house. But a strange thing happened to her as winter passed. When she went upstairs after an evening with Bascombe, she found that reading for an hour before going to bed was restful and, the more she read, the more she wanted to read. She began choosing books with care, and reading on the nights she stayed home. The public library had a fair history section, mostly American and European, with a few titles on ancient Greece and Rome. Ellen read the history of the Civil War by James Truslow Adams, and before she knew it, she was digging into the history of America, moving west until she found herself reading about the very ground she lived on. She began to mix novels into the history and discovered Booth Tarkington, Willa Cather, Sinclair Lewis, and Kenneth Roberts, to mention a few of the authors she read that winter. One April evening, lying beside Bascombe, wondering how he kept it up the way he did, she asked if he liked to read.

"Sure, when I have time."

"What?"

"Morning paper."

"Books?"

"Naw," Bascombe said cheerfully. "Not enough time."

Ellen took his words to mean that books represented a world he had no wish to explore—not that he mistrusted books; he lived for the moment. By that time they understood each other. In all honesty, Bascombe had a natural instinct for her moods. He could come into the apartment, embrace her, undress her, and by the time they finished making love, know whether she was out of sorts or yearning for something he did not understand but felt sympathy for, all with a minimum of words and a good deal of intuition.

Such was not her case. Bascombe did not talk about his business. He had no fear she would sell him out to the pro agents, but, like most men, he automatically concealed business details from women. Bascombe was perfectly willing to talk casually about bootlegging, but Ellen learned nothing beyond the fact that Dave McGonigle had retired because of a weakened heart caused by influenza, and what the lawyer was expected to do for Bascombe in case he was arrested. She did not care; his reticence was unimportant. He was kind and always understanding when she failed to keep a date. Through the winter, seeing him in all stages of dignity from fully dressed to goose-pimpled nakedness, she began to understand him better. He was a study in paradox: kind but always fighting a quick-flaring temper; clean and well-dressed but forgetting to shine his shoes and get his hair cut. When he shaved with a straight-edge razor, he always nicked his face and repeated the hoary joke about the barber who was unable to shave himself cleanly because he could not figure out how to lie down and stand up at the same time.

ONE GLOOMY MARCH morning, Mr. Rosenzweig looked over the top of his glasses at Ellen Kellner and said, "Don't go with traveling men."

Ellen had learned to nod and go on with whatever she was doing whenever Mr. Rosenzweig said something for no apparent reason, but this time she felt that she had to answer.

"I don't, Mr. Rosenzweig."

"All right, if that's the way you want it, but don't say I never warned you."

Later that morning, Mrs. Rosenzweig came to the office and plumped down in the swivel chair behind her desk and began fanning her face with a handful of invoices. She fanned herself in January or July, whether it was ten above or ninety in the shade, and her fine dark brown eyes never lost one ray of cynicism. She looked across the office at Ellen and smiled rather grimly.

"Mr. Rosenzweig meant well."

"Ma'am?"

"What he told you about traveling men. He didn't mean to offend you."

"He didn't, Mrs. Rosenzweig."

"It's true. Don't go with traveling men."

"I don't."

"Hah!" Mrs. Rosenzweig said softly. "That's not a lie because you are not a lying woman, but you have been seeing that man for quite a while, haven't you?"

There were occasions when the world tumbled down around self-satisfied egos in less time than it took the soundless debris to raise the dust. Ellen looked at Mrs. Rosenzweig, her mind groping frantically through the spent months—not the nights, but the days when sunlight shone impartially on saints and sinners, exposing both to the world. If the Rosenzweigs knew about Jack Bascombe, who else knew? Ellen nodded numbly.

"Yes, Mrs. Rosenzweig."

"What do you know about him?"

"Enough."

"See, you are not a liar. I throw cold water in your face, and you have the courage to answer truthfully. But do you know enough?"

"I think so."

"Is he a good man?"

"I don't know," Ellen said. "He's not mean."

"Who does he travel for?"

"He doesn't travel, Mrs. Rosenzweig."

"Then just what does he do?"

"He's a bootlegger."

"Then he is a traveling man!"

"In a way."

"And more respectable than many, believe me, if he sells good liquor."

"I think he does," Ellen said. "I don't drink much."

"Then it must be love."

Ellen sat at her typewriter, hands folded in her lap, asked a question she had never asked herself, much less tried to answer. Mrs. Rosenzweig seemed to read her state of mind.

"Never mind. Is he married?"

"Yes."

"Happily?" Mrs. Rosenzweig rolled her eyes at her own idiocy. "What's happy?"

"I never asked him."

"How long have you been seeing him?"

"A few months—how did you find out, Mrs. Rosenzweig?"

"Say it the way you are thinking it. If we found out, how many others know."

"Yes, that's what I really mean."

"Us? By accident. The woman who told us is a personal friend, not a gossip, but she wanted me to know in case something happened to you. Who else knows? I would say the five of us."

"Five?"

"You, me, Mr. Rosenzweig, my friend, and your bootlegger. My friend asked me to tell you to be more careful when you go in and out. The door squeaks."

Then Ellen knew. Mrs. Rosenzweig's friend lived on the west wing hallway.

"That's right," Mrs. Rosenzweig said, "and she is not a snooper, but late one night she heard a door squeak. She is a widow and afraid of burglars. She opened her door a crack and saw your bootlegger tiptoeing out the back door, then you came from the apartment and went upstairs. Here"—Mrs. Rosenzweig handed Ellen a quarter—"with her compliments, please buy a can of 3-in-1 and use it, so she can sleep and not dream of when she too was young."

Five

RETURNING FROM BENT Fork one warm afternoon in June, the lumberman and his wife were shaken from their pleasant reverie by the sound of something he thought at first was a runaway locomotive that rushed up behind their Nash, sounded a deep, throaty horn, and passed them in a flurry of thrown gravel. They saw the vague shape of a big car that disappeared over the next rise before they could identify more than an off-gray color with a silvery gleam.

"Good God!" the lumberman said, spitting dust. "What was that?"

He slowed down to let the dust settle before resuming the sedate thirty-five-mile-an-hour speed that brought them into Cherrygrove without further shock from headless horsemen. His wife said, "We need milk," and when he parked outside the general store, they saw the big car in front of the drugstore, surrounded by grownups and children. It was silver-gray and even in repose it had a mean look of being poised on the brink of mile-a-minute speeds over all roads in all kinds of weather. His wife went into the store for milk, and returned with the latest gossip.

"It's a Graham-Paige," she reported. "Bascombe just bought it."

"I saw the ads. Lots of aluminum in it."

"Why?"

"Makes it lighter." The lumberman's eyes twinkled. "Should be brass."

His wife pursed her lips in approbation, not at him, but the bootlegger. It was just like Bascombe to pay a great deal of money for a fast car at the same time everybody else was hurting in the pocketbook. As far as she could determine, no one in town had bought a new car since Christmas of 1929. Even her husband, who could easily afford to trade, was still driving their 1928 sedan.

BASCOMBE'S NEW CAR was the talk of the town ten minutes after he parked in front of the drugstore and hurried inside to take care of any barbering that had piled up during his absence. He was filled with an ineffable sense of importance, knowing that he had bought and paid for a car so sensational in design and looks that it was bound to be a flop before the first one sold. Bascombe fiddled with his barber tools, washed his hands, and went back to the soda fountain for a glass of water. He could hardly wait to show the car to Ellen and tell her his plans for the summer; meanwhile, he strolled outside and gave the crowd a cheery hello as he got behind the wheel, hit the starter, and watched them jump at the sound of the powerful engine. He backed out and drove home, bundled his wife and child into the front seat, and took them for a ride in the country. His wife waited until they returned to bore straight to the gist of his folly.

"How much did it cost?"

"The dealer was stuck with it."

"I'll bet he was!"

"The old Ford was on its last legs," Bascombe argued reasonably, "and you know I need a car that can get up and go. This baby fills the bill."

She could not refute that central truth of a bootlegger's life. After supper, Bascombe packed a grip and told her he was going north to see a man about a horse. He drove ten miles before swinging west and south, and was late arriving at the apartment house. It was past nine o'clock when he unlocked the door and found

Ellen lying on the bed in her slip, reading a magazine and sipping a glass of iced tea. Bascombe had meant to take her for a joyride, but the sight of her on the bed made him forget the car. They knew each other so well that no words were wasted. They made love with unabated interest and enjoyment until both fell back and stared at the ceiling, floating in that blue meadow of suspended time when the mind was blank and the body exhausted. Finally, Bascombe raised up on one elbow and said, "I got a new car today."

"What kind?"

Bascombe tried to speak with casual offhandedness: "A Graham-Paige."

Ellen knew quite a lot about automobiles from reading the ads. Bascombe had unerringly picked the one automobile that practically guaranteed their future loss of anonymity.

"Listen," Bascombe went on, "do you think you can get a couple of weeks off this summer?"

"I don't know."

"Give it a try," Bascombe said. "I've got a great idea."

"What?"

"Let's take a trip."

"Where?"

"Kansas City."

BASCOMBE SAID, "WHERE are we?"

Ellen opened the road map and checked the name of the town they had just entered.

"Mound City."

"How far to go?"

"A little over ninety miles."

"That's a breeze!"

Bascombe took a fresh grip on the big steering wheel. The Graham-Paige growled as he pressed the footfeed and left Mound City, Missouri, behind. Ellen's stomach felt queasy and her eyes hurt from staring through the bug-splattered windshield at the highway rushing under the hood; it was ten o'clock on a hot Sunday morning and the speedometer registered fifty-five miles an hour. She wondered what Bascombe would do when they hit the pavement nearer Kansas City.

Ellen's vacation did not officially begin until the next day, but Bascombe had suggested she take the midnight milk train on Saturday, the twenty-second, and get into Omaha early Sunday morning, where he'd meet her and they would head for Kansas City. Ellen had not believed she could get two weeks off, but Mrs. Rosenzweig said, "Business is so bad, you might as well let us worry," and gave her a week's vacation with pay, starting on Monday, August twenty-fourth. Ellen told her sister that she had always dreamed of taking a trip by herself, once she reached her twenty-first birthday, and it was now or never. She had saved enough money to take the milk train to Omaha, ride a morning local south to Capitol City, stay at the YWCA, visit the celebrated state capitol building, the university, and other historical spots.

Twila helped her pack and saw her off at midnight on Saturday. Ellen took a seat in the first day-coach on the platform side, opened both windows, and leaned out to say goodbye. When the bell rang and the steam blew, Twila held on to her hat, looked up, and said, "Don't let him drive that Graham-Paige too fast," and the train moved out, leaving Ellen at the window, smelling smoke and soot, wondering how and when her sister had found out.

She dozed most of the way to Omaha and got down at five-thirty in the morning with all the other sleepy-eyed passengers who hefted their grips and went up the platform, climbed the stairs, and crossed the station rotunda to the street. Ellen came through the revolving door onto the sidewalk, and there was Bascombe, just as he had planned and promised, standing beside the Graham-Paige at the end of the taxi line. He stowed her grip in the backseat, opened the right front door, and took her elbow. As she gathered the back of her skirt and got into the car, Ellen saw a young girl come from the station with a suitcase in both hands, evidently just off the milk train. Ellen looked at the girl, who could be her, in the same moment the girl's eyes widened at sight of the Graham-Paige. Then Bascombe pulled from the curb and the girl was lost in traffic.

ELLEN RETURNED FROM her vacation on Sunday, September third. The first words she spoke to her sister were, "How did you find out?"

One night early in August, Twila explained, she was late taking the garbage downstairs. A hot summer wind was blowing as she walked along the garage line toward the garbage can rack; it banged open the doors of the end garage and she saw the rear of a big silver-gray Graham-Paige bearing the license 27-798. Blackbird County's license number was 27. Twila had heard several stories about Jack Bascombe's Graham-Paige; if this was his car, what in the world was it doing here? Twila deposited her garbage and walked up front to the lobby mailboxes; the apartment that corresponded to the garage number bore the name of Smith.

Twila had a premonition, but refused to jump to conclusions. She wrote the Blackbird County clerk's office, requesting the name of the owner of a Graham-Paige bearing the license 27-798. In due time she received a reply stating that license plate 27-798 was registered to Jack Bascombe of Cherrygrove. The next time Ellen went to the library after supper, Twila waited fifteen minutes and followed. Ellen was not in the library; on her way home, Twila detoured past the garages and found the Graham-Paige in the end stall.

Even so, she wanted to be absolutely sure. The next time Ellen left for the library after supper, Twila went downstairs and checked the end garage; the Graham-Paige was inside. Twila waited in the darkness until, a few minutes later, Ellen came off the side street and went up the back steps into the west wing hallway. Twila waited five minutes before going upstairs; their apartment was empty.

Twila bided her time until she saw Ellen off on vacation.

Standing on the platform, she looked up at her sister and deliberately waited until the bell rang before she exploded what surely would be a bombshell. And now Ellen shook her head.

"I knew that damn car would spoil everything."

"Don't tell me you thought it would last forever?"

Ellen smiled sheepishly. "I'm not that dumb."

"Then what *did* you think?"

"I don't know . . . nothing—don't we all?"

Twila's smile was a trifle grim; she had been seeing the same traveling man twelve times a year for seven years. What was *she* thinking?

BROWN LEAVES WARMED the cold earth, fall deepened. On the day before Thanksgiving, Ellen stood in the shop entrance with Mrs. Rosenzweig, watching the Homecoming Parade pass by. The coach rode in the lead convertible, waving to the crowd, looking older and tireder, obligatory smiles fewer by the block. Mrs. Rosenzweig had never, by word or action, let on that she knew the coach, so her sudden remark came as a surprise.

"Poor man, so much to offer, to give so little . . . don't you know him?"

"Yes," Ellen said. "He was coach when I was in school."

"Then you must know."

"Know what?"

Mrs. Rosenzweig uttered her customary snort that signified secret knowledge, disdain, disgust, or some other more subtle shade of emotion that always seemed to match the glint in her dark eyes. Her snort varied from a "Hah!" to a "Humph!" to the Homecoming "Hoo!" that preceded her words. "Such a big, strong man. A good mind too, and what does he use it for? To win games when he should be winning battles."

"Battles?"

"The battles of life," Mrs. Rosenzweig said impatiently. "You don't grow up when you win games, you just win games! And that's not all."

"What else could there be, Mrs. Rosenzweig?"

"It explains better in Yiddish," Mrs. Rosenzweig said, "but just for you, I'll try to make a literal translation. Have you ever known the Don Juan, the Casanova, the ladykiller who always dates the Homecoming Queen? Every year the idiot is one year older, and the Homecoming Queen is always eighteen. How long can he go on, eh?"

"But the coach never dates Homecoming Queens."

"Did I say *he* did? He does other things. It is lucky he wins games, otherwise he might not stay. Well, back to work!"

On the following afternoon, Bent Fork High School defeated Capitol City 13 to 6, extending their winning streak to twenty-eight games over four full seasons, three victories short of tying the all-time state record set by Capitol City during the years 1916 to 1920, under the coaching of the man who was now director of athletics for the entire Capitol City school system. The coach who broke that splendid record would become a marked man, known and noticed by larger schools in cities from the Mississippi to the Rocky Mountains.

Six

W INTER WAS FILLED with life's hard knocks, and spring was no better. Many people had that *on your mark, get set, go* look of someone poised to leap from danger; their chances would have improved if only they had known in which direction safety lay. They bought coal by the sackful instead of the ton, made things last, or did without; conditions were worse in the eastern cities, and so many people were going west that it seemed as if California might grow top-heavy and tip into the Pacific Ocean. The president and Congress did nothing to help, big business did less, and farm prices hit rock bottom. Nobody knew what was going to happen, least of all the politicians who were getting ready for the big conventions. By the time they chose the candidates, everything that could happen would have happened, and there was only one way to go and that was up, but how did you rise without means of ascension?

Conditions worsened as spring wore into summer. Banks kept failing, stocks hit a new low, the Republican National Convention renominated Herbert Hoover and tried to sound enthusiastic about the selection, refusing to admit publicly that nobody else wanted the honor. People asked who was this fellow named Roosevelt, nominated by the Democrats, some relative of the late Theodore? Everybody waited impatiently for the opening of the presidential campaign on Labor Day; and closer to home, the Cherrygrove town board threw a curve at Jack Bascombe. The pavilion dances were nearly out of hand, and two changes were announced. The marshal would swear in special deputies to stand duty during all dances, and bootleggers would not be allowed on the premises. Then the county sheriff promised that his deputies would patrol all adjacent roads on dance nights, to keep bootleggers as far from the pavilion as possible.

Bascombe spent the month of August racking his brain for some way of piercing the wall that had chopped off an easy part of his business. He was so intent on solving the problem that for the first time in their relationship he forgot to undress Ellen when he entered the apartment the evening of the announcement by the town board. Ellen wisely said nothing, and offered no suggestions. She could have mentioned that she had known, for some time, that the mood of the country was changing to match the conservative atmosphere of the Depression. There was no better place than a dress shop to anticipate shifts in public style and opinion, and both had plainly decreed the end of flappers, shapeless frocks, chopped-off hair, and Clara Bow mouths. Wholesome figures bloomed, hemlines dropped below the knee, and hair actually covered the nape of the neck. Ellen had never bobbed her hair, exaggerated her mouth with lipstick, or confined her breasts under silly dresses. She held her tongue until Bascombe reverted to his normal condition; later in the evening he sat up in bed and swore with soft finality.

"Damn, there's no way!"

Ellen woke. "What's wrong?"

"I can't do it."

Bascombe was finally showing a few signs of common sense. Ellen rubbed his back and tried to speak soothingly. "No use taking unnecessary chances."

"You're right."

"Things are changing."

"What things?"

"Well, Prohibition for one. Don't you think they'll repeal the Eighteenth Amendment?"

"Naw," Bascombe said. "Not for a long time."

ROOSEVELT SHOWED THAT he had not taken his convention speech promises lightly. He opened the campaign with a rousing reitera-tion of everything he intended to do. As the days passed and he met the issues head-on with short, clear statements of intent, peo-ple realized that his ideas made sense. That fact alone was unique in a presidential campaign. He talked about what had to be done, not what ought to be tried. There was a world of difference in harping on the fact that government was legally restrained from helping hungry, jobless, homeless, sick people, and saying bluntly that government *must* step in, *must* do everything humanly possi-ble to end a state of emergency unprecedented in the nation's his-tory. Roosevelt had a wonderful voice on the radio, and all his newspaper and newsreel pictures showed him smiling, his cigaret holder canted upward from the corner of his mouth like a flag that didn't know the meaning of half-mast. He could joke, and laugh, and somehow reach out to people in a way that rekindled hopes and dreams.

Campaigning on the other side of the fence, Hoover appeared to fear his own good thoughts. Nobody Ellen knew seemed to doubt that he was concerned about the country, but nobody be-lieved he would do anything about putting the vast, unlimited re-sources of the government to work for the good of the people. He had always gone precisely by the rule book; his speeches were as dry as the ink delineating his exceptional record of organization and efficiency compiled during a lifetime of unquestioned service to his employers. He could, and had, moved mountains, given the time to make neat plans and issue orders to other neat, efficient people who had the skills to transport raw materials and supplies from one place to another. If only he had a heart!

Ellen could not remember a more exciting campaign in her short life. Older people made comparisons with 1912, the Bull

Moose battle, but others reminded them that twenty years ago the country was in good shape and the fight was among Teddy, William Howard, and Woodrow, who did not face the problems of finding food and work for millions. There was no radio in 1912; had there been, Mr. Rosenzweig swore, Theodore Roosevelt likely would have won the election, because he was a stemwinder when he got wound up. Franklin D. Roosevelt was a new chip off that old Dutch burgher block, blessed with a smoother tongue and a real feeling for the common man. There was no doubt in Ellen's mind when she stepped into the booth to vote for the first time on Tuesday, November first; and early the next morning the radio announced that Franklin Delano Roosevelt was elected the thirty-second president of the United States.

THE COACH CAST his vote for Roosevelt, and returned to the serious business at hand. On Friday, his team won its thirty-third consecutive football game; two weeks later the season ended with the thirty-fifth victory. Five straight seasons without defeat was still a long way from the national record, but viewed in the perspective of achievement for a high school in a town of ten thousand, willing to play the biggest schools it could schedule, made the difference to knowledgeable football fans—and more important, to certain booster clubs in larger cities, who never stopped looking for the perfect coach.

The coach was far from perfect, but he had changed inwardly. He had stopped seducing graduating seniors and contracted more mature alliances that seldom lasted longer than a few months before his enthusiasm cooled and sent him off on the eternal search for whatever it was he sought in a woman. His longtime friend, the lawyer, approved the inward change while wondering how much longer Bent Fork could hold the man who had become a superb teacher of football, who at the same time grew more mature with each passing season. The lawyer made no brief for athletic maturity; it ranked far beneath maturity in other fields of human endeavor. And yet!

What was the final result? Were the standout people in art, literature, music, business, education, religion, and the professions more successful in the long run than the man who, surprisingly, had changed himself while working to shape young men in some mythical mold that surely had its origin in those lost Greek ages when body and mind were deemed on a par, and brought to twin peaks of mutual triumph over mind and matter? The lawyer explained his supposition to the coach one evening, and the coach surprised the lawyer by not only agreeing in principle, but admitting that he had entertained similar thoughts, not for the purpose of self-admiration, but from the standpoint of trying to make his players understand the principles of strong body–strong mind. The lawyer shook his head in wonder.

"By God, I never thought you had it in you!"

"For all the good it does me," growled the coach. "Just tell me one thing."

"Name it."

"Who's going to play left half next season? That, by God, is the question!"

"Ask Gertrude."

"Gertrude?"

"Come on," the lawyer said jovially. "Let's go somewhere and lift a stein."

Seven

MARCH FOURTH FELL on a snowy Saturday that year. It was the first time Ellen Kellner heard the oath of office administered to a president-elect by the Chief Justice of the Supreme Court. She sat in the office with the Rosenzweigs and listened intently as Roosevelt repeated the oath and then gave his inaugural address. It was one of those times during which many people knew, just knew, that they were actually a part of what history really was, something that happened to all of them in the same instant, and gave them all a strange feeling of elation mixed with inexplicable sadness when Roosevelt told them—and it was true, everybody listening felt he was talking to *them*—that the only thing they had to fear was fear itself. Ellen remembered nothing else from the speech but that one sentence, and evidently everybody else remembered it too, because people seemed to perk up that day, shake off part of the blues, and act like conditions were bound to improve within the week.

The truth was, conditions got worse but somehow seemed a little better, even on March sixth when Roosevelt declared a bank holiday that closed every bank in the country for four days and gave the tottering financial system time to get back on its feet. Congress passed emergency legislation that empowered the Federal Reserve System and the Reconstruction Finance Corporation to help sound banks with infusions of new currency.

Roosevelt reported these acts in another radio broadcast on Sunday evening, March twelfth, and the next morning people began redepositing their money. To Ellen, the most surprising part of the whole business was that despite the gloomy predictions of ruin and revolution, the scheme actually worked.

But that early success was about all that did work. Farms were still on the block, business had slowed to a crawl, and the die-hard Prohibitionists were sorrowing over the imminent passage of what would become the Twenty-first Amendment to the Constitution and repeal the Eighteenth Amendment as soon as it was ratified by thirty-six states. The way public sentiment had shifted away from Prohibition, it was a cinch to become law by the end of 1933. It took a man of vision to believe in the future of bootlegging; Jack Bascombe surely had to be considered a visionary because he not only applauded Roosevelt, but apparently refused to face the truth. One night in April, when a sensible man would have been planning his new future, Bascombe said, "You know what I like best about you?"

Ellen roused herself. "What?"

"You don't nag."

"Why should I? We're not married."

Bascombe ingested the earth-shaking simplicity of a great truth stumbled upon blindly. He was wise enough not to pursue the question to greater depth by asking Ellen if she wanted to get married. He believed, with wholehearted honesty, that she was like him in all respects. Ellen did not try to enlighten him, nor did she thrust an oblique thought into his right-angled mind by explaining how she felt every time a young wife entered the shop to buy a maternity dress. Bascombe had the natural intuition to follow up his compliment with a new plan of action.

"Can you get a week off in May?"

"I don't know—why?"

"Because I've got a helluva idea," Bascombe said, and told her what he intended to do. He was going to Chicago, where he could buy a carload of alcohol for twenty-five percent less than he paid the delivery man from the north; it was worth the trip, which should be a fine vacation for both of them. Ellen could take the night train to Sioux City where he would pick her up, and go on to Chicago. "Well, what do you think?"

Ellen asked the question every bootlegger should put to himself. "Do you know these people?"

"Sure I know them."

"I mean, can you trust them?"

"Jesus Christ!" Bascombe said. "We're in the same line of work."

"But why would they sell you the same goods for twenty-five percent less?"

"Maybe they get it cheaper at the other end," Bascombe said. "Maybe they've got too much stock. Who cares? Their man came through here last week and quoted me a firm price if I can get there before the end of May."

"I don't know—"

"Make up your mind," Bascombe said. "Either way, I go no later than May fifteenth."

Ellen had spent the winter thinking about her future. One of Bascombe's virtues was keeping his promises, but he had been thwarted time and again that winter by the weather; then his wife came down with the croup and he had to take care of the house and their child for two weeks. With time on her hands, Ellen considered her present state, and her possible future, while spending more time at the library, taking more books home, and looking at herself in the mirror. If she had a wrinkle, it was under the skin; if she was happy, that too was hidden. How long did this magical time last? She was lucky and—well, she had never seen Chicago.

JACK BASCOMBE LEFT for Chicago on May twelfth, the day Congress passed the Agricultural Adjustment Act. Late in the day, Ellen Kellner caught the train for Sioux City. She stepped into the ladies' washroom a minute before the train stopped in Cherrygrove and did not return to her seat until it was halfway to Burnside. She banked on the fact that Cherrygrove people rarely, if ever, took the late train to Sioux City. She was right; nobody had boarded in Cherrygrove. Bascombe met her in the Sioux City station, put her grip in the backseat, and made her comfortable in front. He went around behind the wheel, opened his wallet, and handed her a thick sheaf of banknotes.

"You keep this."

"I don't want to, Jack."

"Damn it!" Bascombe said. "It's in case something goes haywire."

Nothing went haywire, as he put it, on their drive to Chicago. They checked into a nice hotel, where Bascombe registered as Mr. and Mrs. Bascombe, and nobody gave them a second look. Next morning, while Bascombe went about the serious business of buying alcohol, Ellen had her first chance to see a big city. She walked the streets, wandered through department stores, looked into shop windows, and discovered that Mrs. Rosenzweig was right: Style covered the entire country, and the only difference in current styles was the quality of the material and the work. Shoes and accessories were different in the same way, and the best clothing lines were in the big department stores and the exclusive shops. Ellen lost track of time until she found herself walking in late afternoon shadow; a window clock read ten minutes of six. She took a cab to the hotel, drew a bath, and waited for Bascombe. He returned at eight, cursing the soot that dirtied his collar, but happy to report that the deal was all set. He could load the Graham-Paige any time he chose between now and the day before they left for home.

"So let's have some fun," he said. "We've earned it."

Ellen said, "I'd like to buy some clothes."

"Good Lord, yes," Bascombe said. "That's what the money is for."

"I didn't mean your money, Jack."

"Don't argue," Bascombe said. "You buy clothes, I'll try to find a good barber."

Whereupon he fell on the bed and roared with laughter at his old joke, and the nearest they came to going out was ordering midnight supper and setting the tray of dirty dishes in the hall. But in the days that followed, they did everything that tourists with plenty of money could do in Chicago: eat, drink, attend shows and baseball games, ride the El, take a boat cruise on Lake Michigan, buy clothes, and make love. Ellen made a special trip to the Marshall Field book department and bought a copy of *Anthony Adverse* to read at home. Bascombe bought gifts for his wife and child, and surprised Ellen with a bottle of the best perfume he could find. On the sixth day they ate an early supper, and Bascombe took the car somewhere to be loaded. While he was gone, Ellen did something she had planned several days ago; she sewed almost all the money she had left into her bandeau, put it on, and looked at herself in the mirror. She couldn't see a thing; it was completely hidden. Bascombe returned at eight, paid their hotel bill, and finished packing; they drove from Chicago at ten-thirty. The minute Ellen got into the car, she could feel the difference. The big sedan rode low with the weight of five-gallon cans of alcohol stacked in the backseat and covered with an automobile robe, as if anybody cared what they carried.

She dozed off, woke when Bascombe stopped for a red light, saw the crossing gate and heard the bell, and sleepily counted the passing freight cars. She dozed off again, and much later, in gray morning light, woke to see another red light blinking up ahead. She said, "Crossing?" and Bascombe answered, "Looks like an accident," but it turned out to be a roadblock on the eastern edge of a small town, with cars parked across the highway and policemen swinging bull's-eye lanterns. Bascombe stopped and someone said, "Step out, please," and the fun began.

Eight

I N THOSE PROHIBITION years it was routine procedure for the news agencies to send stories about people in the news to the communities from whence they came; thus, when the law enforcement officers working the roadblock on the east side of a small Illinois city arrested a man and woman driving a fast sedan loaded with alcohol, the local AP man got the facts from the desk sergeant and sent them to his Chicago office. The story reached the *Bent Fork Daily News* in time to make next day's paper. People in Bent Fork and all the towns around read the story on page two, stating that Jack Bascombe of Cherrygrove and Miss Ellen Kellner of Bent Fork had been arrested for transporting a load of alcohol. Subsequent follow-ups requested by the *Daily News* city editor reported that Bascombe's automobile and cargo had been confiscated, he was fined four hundred and thirty-five dollars and given a six-months' jail sentence, while his companion, Miss Kellner, was fined forty-five dollars, given a one-month suspended jail sentence, and released in her own custody.

MRS. BASCOMBE READ the story in her *Daily News*, and wasted no time responding to such stimuli. She telephoned her parents in a river town eighty miles east of Cherrygrove. They arrived at eight o'clock the next morning, bundled her and their grandson into the car, and drove to Bent Fork where they met with a lawyer who exchanged telephone calls with law enforcement officials in the Illinois city to verify the AP story. The lawyer ascertained the amount of Bascombe's fine and the length of his jail sentence, and proceeded with certain legal steps. He employed an obscure codicil to the state law concerning separation and divorcement to draw up papers enabling Mrs. Bascombe to open her husband's safe deposit box in the Bent Fork First National Bank and do as she wished with the contents. Nobody knew what she found; the guesses ranged from one to ten thousand dollars. Whatever it was, Mrs. Bascombe packed and shipped her personal belongings and household goods, and departed Cherrygrove to start divorce proceedings in her old hometown.

THE COACH'S FIRST impulse was the typical anger of a proud man who discovered that the woman he turned from, for humanitarian reasons, had not become a nun. Then the coach cursed himself bitterly for such selfish behavior, and visited his lawyer friend. He said, "What will they do to her?" and the lawyer said, "Nothing."

"Did you know about them?"

"No," the lawyer said. "Honest to God, I didn't!"

"You know him?"

"Legally."

"Good God!" the coach said. "A client?"

"A *good* client," the lawyer amended. "Paid his fees promptly, never bothered me with trifles, never asked a favor he couldn't repay."

"What kind of man is he?"

"In some ways," the lawyer said, "a good deal like you."

The coach raised his arms in supplication. "What'll happen to him?"

"Confiscation of car and alcohol, fined every cent in his pockets, jail sentence."

"And her?"

"Same in-pocket fine and a suspended sentence."

"Is there anything I can do for her?"

"Not a thing," the lawyer said, "unless you want to go back there and get *your* name in the funny papers."

The coach looked at the framed diplomas on the wall behind the lawyer's desk, and wondered what would happen to him if he hurried to that Illinois town, openly admitted his friendship with a kept woman, offered to pay her fine or be her character witness, do whatever the law required to ease her trouble and help her out of a situation that was so common it would be forgotten five minutes after she left the courtroom—and with luck, fifty years after she was gone from Cherrygrove and Bent Fork. Against that array of facts, despite holding the record for the longest winning streak in high school football, the coach would be lucky if his contract was renewed, let alone receive offers from larger schools. He looked at the proud diplomas and saw himself, framed and cased and dipped in bronze, idolized and praised and paid good money to win something as unimportant as football games played by sterling young men who had probably seduced more young women than the barber.

"If it would help her," he said, "I'd leave now."

"Treasure the thought," the lawyer said, "and sit on your hands. She'll come out all right."

"How do you know?"

"Because I have already sent telegrams at the bequest of my clients."

"Your clients?"

"I do not believe I am betraying a confidence," the lawyer said, "in telling you that the afternoon the story ran in the *Daily News*, Mr. and Mrs. Rosenzweig came here to engage me to do everything in my power to help Ellen. I have done everything, and she should be home soon."

The coach stared at his old friend and shook his head in wonder. "You never know! By God, you never know!"

Nine

G OING THROUGH THE motions of living that summer, Ellen Kellner thought how she seemed to go from one extreme to the other, from a man to no men at all, and where would she finally land? People swore that a person could not change; in her case, she knew they were saying: "Once a slut, always a slut!" But she could stand the knowing looks and the dirty thoughts. What she could not bear was the weight of her own consciousness. Her consciousness, not her conscience! If Bascombe had taught her anything, it was the idiocy of basking in her own conscience. If you decided to do something, and did it, you had no right to fall back on conscience as an easy way out. If you sinned, as her condition was described for some ancient, so-called civilized reason that was nearer cruelty than kindness, you were supposed to beg forgiveness from some invisible source, and thus be purified.

The fallacy of that argument was that she did not feel the need for purification. She hadn't done anything that was not humanly normal, so why go through the public motions of acting contrite and begging forgiveness from an unseen force she did not understand because she had never seen it, felt it, or needed it? But having gone through the entire litany, she still felt the weight of her own consciousness. Thank God, she had all summer to wrestle with the problem, and she got so wrapped up in examining herself that she forgot to be penitent and meek, and went about her business as though nothing had happened. But she did one thing the day after she returned. She took the money out of her bandeau, three hundred and sixty dollars in twenty-dollar bills, put it in an envelope, and took it to the lawyer. It was the first time she had talked to him since the coach kissed her goodbye. She asked him to please give the envelope to Bascombe when he came home.

The lawyer counted the money and wrote her a receipt. "Now seal it in the envelope."

Ellen licked and sealed. "And tell him I don't want to see him again."

"I will," the lawyer said. "More important right now, can I do anything for you?"

"No, but thank you."

Ellen returned to her job at the dress shop, where the only thing Mrs. Rosenzweig said was, "I ought to give away one chance with every fifty-dollar purchase," and when Ellen said, "On what?" Mrs. Rosenzweig said, "On you," but gave away her concern with her smile. All Mr. Rosenzweig ever said was, "Traveling men!" and gave her a little pat on the shoulder. Toward summer's end, Ellen decided that she had done the right things: returned what was left of the money, and broken the relationship for good. She was not angry at Bascombe, nor was she angry with herself. It was just that she could once more live with her own consciousness, a condition that had come to mean her own awareness of what she was doing, why she did it, and where she wanted to go as a result. Not *go,* but *wanted* to go. She had no idea where the end was, or how she had to travel to get there, but she had to go on, and going with Bascombe was not the way. It was better for her, and for him, never to see each other again. She did not mean it in the romantic sense of lovers forever parted; she did not mean it in the dream of finding legal love, whatever that was. She had to find a way that held more promise than going to bed, or the reverse, a kind of platonic association, or a life with someone who had no capacity for talking and thinking, reading books, sharing a few ideas, helping her unravel her tangled thoughts. What she needed was a miracle, and just when she had enough of her summer calefactory, Labor Day passed and the first cool evening breeze touched her face on the long walk home.

BASCOMBE RETURNED TO Bent Fork early in November on the morning passenger from Omaha. He got down at the south-side station and walked the mile north to the lawyer's office on Bent Fork Avenue. The lawyer shook hands and sat him in one of the brown leather chairs that made a sharp contrast to Bascombe's pale skin and the feeling that seemed to come quivering out of the inner man. Bascombe said, "You wrote to come straight here. What for?"

The lawyer took an envelope from his safe and handed it across the desk. "Open it, please, and count the money."

Bascombe opened the envelope and counted out three hundred and sixty dollars in twenty-dollar bills. He looked up in honest perplexity. "I never left any money with you."

"Miss Kellner gave it to me, the day after she got home."

"My God!" Bascombe said. "I thought they got it too."

"She told me she sewed it inside her bandeau the night before you left Chicago. They missed it when they searched her."

"Did she lose her job?"

"Of course not!"

"I'm glad to hear that. I've got to thank her—"

"No," the lawyer said firmly. "You put her through a wringer, Jack. She wants to be left alone. Promise?"

Bascombe seemed to shrink inside himself, not so much mentally or physically as sexually. "All right."

"Thank you, Jack. I knew you'd respect her wish."

"I guess that's it then?"

"Yes—not going to bootleg again, are you?"

"No."

"It's nearly finished anyway. What are you going to do?"

"Haven't made up my mind."

"Don't worry, you've got a good trade to fall back on. And if I can ever do anything, come see me."

"Thanks," Bascombe said. "You've been on the up and up with me all the way. A man couldn't ask for more."

The lawyer bent his head in appreciation. "Thank *you*, Jack."

Bascombe turned at the door. "Want to ask me, don't you?"

"What?"

"If I wised up to how they took me?"

"Did you wise up?"

"Sure, too damn late! It's a nice little deal between those Chicago birds and the locals in all the towns around Chicago. One of the deputies told me they work it all the time. The alcohol goes back to Chicago, and the locals split the fines and whatever cash they get from selling the car." Bascombe grinned wryly, and a ray of his old spirit broke through the jail pallor. "Well, it was fun while it lasted."

Bascombe showed up in Cherrygrove two days later, driving an old Dodge pickup. He collected his personal belongings, his barber chair and tools, and left town. Someone remarked, "How the mighty have fallen," and it was easy to believe that Bascombe had gone to pieces, but two weeks later Henry Lang stopped in Hurrah, a one-horse town seven miles west of Cherrygrove on the Bent Fork River, a village of less than fifty people become practically a ghost town in the Depression. Henry Lang parked in front of a faded barber pole and stuck his head through the doorway to inquire directions to a farmer who wanted to sell several cows, and there, sitting in the chair, reading the paper, was Bascombe.

"Hello, Jack," Henry said. "I didn't know you were over here."

"Hello, Henry," Bascombe said. "Shave, haircut?"

Was this the end of dreams, easy money, Graham-Paige, girl? It appeared that Bascombe was trying to sink into oblivion, but Henry Lang told his close friends that it wasn't true because he had taken Bascombe down the street to the pool hall for a bottle of pop, and after describing how it felt to lie in jail for six months, Bascombe said, "It's a skin game they play on hicks like me. I guess

I better stay a hick," and that was the last time he ever spoke of it to anyone. He had not cursed fate, taken to the bottle, or given up the ghost. He was simply living on terms with himself, doing the best he could in a world that did not give two cents whether he lived or died.

Ten

A T THE END of a long winter and a spring that dragged cruelly toward summer, the coach watched his graduating quarterback go up the stairs from the locker room, and silently cursed his inability to help solve the boy's problem. The state university coaching staff had a hard and fast rule regarding the recipients of their precious athletic scholarships. The quarterback was not big enough, fast enough, and tall enough to qualify. The schools that wanted him—the teachers' college conference, the denominational conference, and three small private colleges—offered no athletic scholarships. The quarterback's father was a hardworking railroad man who simply did not have the money to send his oldest son to college. The quarterback was one of those athletes who had given four years of dedicated effort to the premise that touchdowns were time-proof and cheers never died. God help them when they came down to earth. The coach did his best to make them understand, but how often had he succeeded? With luck, perhaps a dozen times in his career. There was nothing he could do to change the system; and the bitter truth, coppering his taste at the very moment of his personal triumph, was a grim reminder of the lasting worth of fame.

The coach shrugged and ran up the stairs, jumped into his Model A, drove uptown, and found a parking place in front of Wurlitzer's jewelry store. He went next door into Rosenzweig's

Dress Shop, took off his hat to Mrs. Rosenzweig, and explained his purpose: Back in his old hometown, his oldest sister's oldest daughter was graduating from high school, and he wanted to surprise her with something different, namely "—for her senior prom, the best dress you've got, can you help me?"

Mrs. Rosenzweig said, "We can try," and began showing him those gowns specifically designed for young ladies of eighteen. While she took the gowns off the rack, she asked pertinent questions. The coach answered in general terms. Not good enough! Mrs. Rosenzweig demanded accuracy in weight, height, critical measurements, type of heels, hair color and style, color of eyes and skin, teeth. The coach shook his head at his appalling ignorance, and suddenly snapped his fingers.

"Wait a minute, I've got it!"

"Eh?"

"What we need is a model."

"Your niece's size."

"Does Ellen still work here?"

"Of course."

"Well, my niece is a dead ringer for Ellen in shape and height. Even her hair, come to think of it, she wears it the way Ellen does, down to the shoulders in that what do you call it?"

"Pageboy."

"That's it! I know Ellen's not a model, but do you think she'd put on a dress we pick so we can see how it looks?"

"I'll see," Mrs. Rosenzweig said, sober as a judge and twice as impartial, and raised her voice politely. "Ellen?"

Ellen Kellner appeared in the office doorway. She looked at the coach while Mrs. Rosenzweig explained, and the coach looked at her and felt the same rush of barely governable emotion he had experienced every time he saw her during the past year. His feeling had nothing to do with wanting her in bed, but rather had become a strange growing tenderness that yearned to hold her in a permanent embrace. He did not fully understand himself, but he trusted his own intuition, and the way he felt, he realized that he had been blind to the greater part of Ellen's beauty, the kind that developed as slowly as the girl herself grew out of youth into a womanly maturity that deserved more than making love in a river cabin.

"—I said, how do you like it?"

Mrs. Rosenzweig's voice finally punctured the self-spun fog that enveloped the coach like a cloud of remorse. He had woolgathered while Ellen took the gown Mrs. Rosenzweig selected, stepped into a dressing room, and now stood before him, wearing it in the way his niece could never fill the bill at graduation age. Ellen made no effort to pose or walk or execute artful tricks of salesmanship; she stood in the open space before the full-length triple mirrors and looked at him across twelve feet of rose-colored carpet. The coach found his voice.

"That's it!"

"It will be ready tomorrow noon," Mrs. Rosenzweig said. "Is that too late?"

"No," the coach said. "That's fine."

"Good," Mrs. Rosenzweig said briskly, and glanced down her nose at her lapel watch. "Closing time, we'll press and pack in the morning. Ellen, after you take it off, why don't you go on home. I'll lock up."

Ellen nodded and returned to the dressing room. The coach followed Mrs. Rosenzweig to the cash register, wrote a check for the dress, and when Ellen came from the office in her street clothes, carrying her pocketbook, he turned with a timid smile, "Can I drive you home, Ellen?"

"Thank you, but it isn't far."

The coach said, "I insist," and gave Mrs. Rosenzweig his warmest smile. "Isn't the customer always right?"

Mrs. Rosenzweig returned his smile with the precision of a diamond cutter who knew exactly where to place the knife and how much force to apply: "That depends on what the customer wants."

The coach smiled gritty appreciation of her delicate thrust. Considering his past, which she evidently was all too familiar with, he richly deserved her reply. His present no longer warranted her suspicions, but how to show his change? He stood helpless, hat in hand, dissolving into the ruins of his newfound self-respect. Ellen saved him.

"All right. Goodnight, Mrs. Rosenzweig."

"Goodnight, Ellen."

The coach opened the front door, followed Ellen outside, and motioned to his Model A parked in front of Wurlitzer's. He helped her into the seat, and when he went around behind the wheel, tried to count the watching faces in the storefront windows and lost the total in the glint of late afternoon sun, shining prismatically against the plate glass. He drove west on Bent Fork Avenue, afraid to speak, much less turn his head, tongue-tied when he needed eloquence. Ellen spoke when they rattled over the railroad tracks.

"Isn't this foolish of you?"

"Why?"

"Driving me home, with my reputation? Half the town saw us."

"They can tell the other half," the coach said. "That'll make it unanimous."

Ellen twisted the knife. "But this is your busy time of year. All class sponsors are knee-deep in rings, pictures, yearbooks, sneak day, the prom."

"I haven't gone to the prom in years. I came to Rosenzweigs to see you."

"Not for the dress?"

"It gave me a good excuse."

"You knew how I wore my hair."

"You were listening," the coach said. "Of course I knew. I came for the dress because I want to tell you something."

"After so much trouble, please do!"

"I got an offer two weeks ago," the coach said. "From one of the Denver high schools. A big increase in salary, coach football and basketball, and I don't have to teach civics. I couldn't turn it down. I told the superintendent the same day I got the offer, and he's been kind enough not to tell the papers until this afternoon. I wanted you to know first."

"Congratulations," Ellen said, "and I really mean that, but why tell me first?"

The coach swallowed a lump of fear that felt bigger than a football. He parked in the shade of the big elm tree at the rear corner of the apartment house.

"Listen," he said. "I've been thinking about this for a long time, ever since I knew the offer was bound to come. Damn it, what I'm trying to say is, will you come with me?"

Ellen Kellner had suffered several violent shocks in her young life. She remembered her father's death as a time of bewildered numbness, and she had been scared witless when she broke her right arm at the age of twelve, for fear it would hang crookedly. The worst shock had come when the man beside her walked out of her life; now she heard the same man invite her to return.

"You want me to go with you?"

"Yes."

"You want me to go to Denver and set up"—anger tore her, years of reading and self-education helped her pronounce the word—"a *ménage!*"

"Oh God!" the coach said. "I'm a clumsy bastard! I want you to marry me, come with me, help me. Please, don't say anything now. Call me when you're ready to tell me."

Ellen felt the words rise in her throat, clamoring to be spoken. She gulped down every one as she got out of the car and ran into the apartment house. She heard his car go down Ninth Street, and all she could think of was the idiocy of it all. Mistress of a home in Denver, doing everything a coach's wife had to do, entertaining faculty members and visiting dignitaries, attending games, constantly in the public eye. Oh, she could do it! She knew she could, there had been a time when she dreamed of such a chance, but she was eighteen then, and everything was possible at eighteen! At twenty-four going on twenty-five? Reality finished the young wife's tale: coach's spouse welcomed, admired, complimented, then burned at the stake when gossip crossed the high plains—and it would cross, they could move to Patagonia and it would eventually arrive, and when it did, the coach would be ruined.

Ellen envisioned the worst before she unlocked her door and stepped into the apartment, so she had nothing left to tell herself but the best part. That took three steps into the kitchen for a glass of water and a steadying hand on the sink. He was crazy, she thought, he had gone stark raving mad. He knew all about her, about Bascombe and the apartment, the trips, jail, everything. He knew it all, and he still had the courage to ask. She went into the living room and sat in the easy chair, facing the north window, clasped her hands in her lap like a little girl, or an old, old lady, and stared unseeing at traffic on the avenue, people walking, spring grass greening under the new leaves. She reached one conclusion: He must love her. He had to, and not in the way they began, but differently, in the same way she had changed and slowly looked at herself.

Eleven

ECISION HAD SEEMED a simple matter of yes or no, but nothing was further from the truth. Ellen spent the last days of May asking herself, What about my sister? and What can I tell the Rosenzweigs? How could she say, "Twila, I'm going to get married and move to Denver," and then trot off, leaving Twila to pay all the apartment rent and living expenses; and yet, those items were the unimportant pieces of the whole.

Twila had always been the leader, by unspoken rule of seniority, but during the past year that position of decision-maker had somehow shifted. Twila was apparently growing tired of the daily grind, even of her friend who stopped faithfully on his rounds, the same kind, steady man who had never promised Twila pie in the sky. He was married, intended to stay married, and made certain, in the very beginning, that Twila clearly understood and accepted the condition. Now Ellen was no longer sure how Twila felt, and that made her own decision doubly difficult. She finally told Twila on Memorial Day, when they were lying around indolently, drinking lemonade and taking lukewarm baths that made them feel cool when they stepped from the tub. Twila did not hesitate in replying.

"Only one thing matters."

"Love?"

"Good God, no!" Twila said. "Do you want to get out of this

town, this country, do something with your life? That's what matters. Are you strong enough to do everything you'll have to do?"

Twila's practicality made Ellen consider all sides of her problem. She felt strong emotion, but was it love? How many women had faced the same decision and coldly weighed the issues, to choose the safer, finer, richer way of life. If being a coach's wife was safer and finer! In the sense of doing numberless small things that made up a fuller existence, she knew it was richer. But was that the end-all? Good Lord! She could go around in circles for years trying to make up her mind. Twila was absolutely right: She had to look at it coldly, make up her mind for her own sake. And yet—?

"What about the apartment?"

Twila snapped, "Damn the apartment!"

"And the expenses?"

"I'll manage."

"Are you sure?"

"Yes, I'm sure!" Twila mimicked. "You know what I'm making. I'll get along."

Ellen murmured, "It's been so long."

Twila did not misunderstand. "Did he say he loves you?"

"I think so."

"Then make up your mind, give him an answer, and don't wait to tell the Rosenzweigs. You owe them too much."

"I know that."

Twila went for a walk in the twilight after supper. Ellen picked up the telephone and called the coach's number for the first time. His voice was unchanged over the phone, "Hello?" and when she said, "This is Ellen," the sudden depth of affection was enough to lift her off the ground.

"Ellen!"

"When can I see you?"

"Don't move," the coach said. "I'll be right over!"

He knocked on the door in less than ten minutes, but he did not try to sweep her off her feet. He smiled and followed her into the apartment, took a chair, and accepted a glass of lemonade.

Ellen took the easy chair, smoothed her skirt and said, "When do you have to be there?"

"By July fifteenth."

"All right."

"All right?"

"I'll marry you, I'll go with you."

The coach set his glass on the coffee table and looked down at his hands. It took him a few seconds to find his voice.

"When do you want to be married?"

"Not here," she said, and knew it sounded wrong. "I mean—"

"I know what you mean," the coach said, "and I thank you, and the hell with that! If you want to be married here, here is where it will be."

"Thank you," Ellen said, "but that's not practical. Let's do it on the way."

"Are you sure?"

"If you are."

"Listen," the coach said. "The Rosenzweigs are fine people, probably the finest in town for my money. You have to give them fair notice. If you want to tell them you're leaving, that's fine with me."

"I'll tell them tomorrow," Ellen said. "One month's notice is fair."

"Yes."

"Then we can leave on July fourth?"

The coach nodded. "There's one more thing."

"What?"

"Do you want me to meet your mother?"

"Not yet," Ellen said firmly. "Twila will tell her we eloped. There's plenty of time later on."

"All right," the coach said. "I just want to be sure everything is exactly the way you want it."

A thought struck Ellen head-on, formed by her slowly developed perception that sliced through the layers of convention and deceit, and laid bare the truth. She hoped she did not have too many of the same, because she wasn't at all certain she had the strength to accept such candor. But she mustered up enough to put it into words.

"It's a big high school?"

"Big, and getting bigger."

"Did they ask if you were married?"

"Matter of fact, they did."

"I thought they preferred married men?"

"Matter of fact, they do, but it wasn't a requisite."

"So they made an exception in your case?"

"Not exactly. I told them I'd been trying to get up enough nerve to pop the question. They said, 'Is it a local girl?' and I said, 'Yes,' and they asked how long I had known her, and I said, 'For years,' and that seemed to satisfy them. I added in all honesty that I didn't know if she'd have me, but I had to take the chance."

"What would they do if you told them the truth?"

"About what?"

"Me."

The coach looked at her and she knew everything was going to be all right. The maze of wrinkles around his eyes crinkled in the laughter he had learned to swallow.

"What do you think they'd do if I told them the truth about me?"

Twelve

ELLEN KELLNER CLEANED out her office desk at noon on July third and took those treasured odds and ends home; now, at six-fifteen, she stood at the front door of the dress shop and tried to find the words to say goodbye. Mr. Rosenzweig kissed her cheek and retreated hastily into the back room, dangerously near tears. Ellen looked at Mrs. Rosenzweig and said, "Are you sure you'll be all right?"

"Yes," Mrs. Rosenzweig said. "We've got to be. You, me, everybody who cares about somebody or something. But don't think we'll forget you."

"I'll never forget you, Mrs. Rosenzweig."

"Naturally," Mrs. Rosenzweig said. "How can you forget beauty and brains in one gorgeous package?" She gave Ellen a sudden, fierce hug and pushed her through the doorway. "Now go, go! And for God's sake, remember what I taught you. Never wear red and green, unless it's your face and the dress."

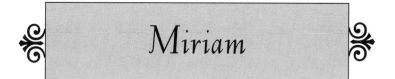

Miriam

One

THE YOUNG GIRLS looked different in the ninth grade. They did something to their hair and dresses and shoes that gave them a look of transparent maturity until noon of the first day of the new school year; then they forgot their masquerade, joined the workup game on the playground, and trooped inside as sweaty, red-faced, and disheveled as they had been a year ago. But school itself was different. Their close-knit group was invaded by outsiders; not really strangers, because their new classmates came from the country schools, but unknown quanities that rasped their comfortable status quo. Harvey Marquardt smelled of damp talcum powder, Walter Kelton hadn't cleaned the horse manure off his shoes, and Vera Stensrud fidgeted in her seat and plucked at her sleeves as if it had taken an act of God to get her into a dress. Why was she that way? She had worn dresses in country school.

It took time to understand that coming to Cherrygrove was as drastic a change for the country students as it was for the graduating Cherrygrove tenth-graders starting the eleventh grade in Bent Fork. They became the outsiders invading a strange, much bigger school, thrust into a closed fraternity that resented newcomers as strongly as the newcomers resented coming. It was an impossible situation that could never be resolved.

Their principal knew better. Years of experience had taught

William Phegley that within the month they would pull together like plow horses. Why not? They came from the same earth, air, and water. They liked the same things, inherited the same ignorances, nursed the same ingrown prejudices; in the course of two years they would become inseparable friends and enemies, part in tears, and go their disparate ways. He knew, too, that on this warm September day in 1930, they were sifting through a bone here, a hank there, trying to make sense of the future that pulled them forward. It was like walking home from school, looking at sidewalk cracks, grass, stones, clouds, sky; jumping a crack, kicking a stone, stepping onto grass, leaping back on cement, acting out a role that was not a figment of imagination but a piece of the day they were spending, trying to discover why they acted as they did, until the act became real and the sidewalk turned into something they no longer recognized, which was to say, it was hard to grow up and tell one another how they felt, not for fear of laughter or jeers, but for fear that each would understand, leaving them all bareminded, with nothing to hold secret for a rainy day inside the heart. And this, in the uncharted sense of exploration, made them all rare creatures.

On that first day of school, William Phegley told them, "You will triumph," and did not add one word to his mysterious salutation. He had a way about him, a quiet aura of black-browed authority that shriveled the pugnacity of every burly country boy who dreamed of challenging the principal. He was one of those surviving auks doomed to vanish from schoolrooms within the next score of years, never to be found again. He could teach two dozen ninth- and tenth-graders all their subjects, in the same room, and make them learn. He taught them the self-discipline needed to close their ears and study while others recited, and he began every school year with one advantage: He knew every child who came up through the grades in Cherrygrove, and most of the students from the country schools.

On the second day he always told them that he did not believe that old saying about watching your entire life pass by your eyes in the split second before death came. He knew a lot of people who could not remember what they did yesterday, let alone their entire lives, but he promised that by the time they graduated from the tenth grade in May 1932, every one of them would be able to remember who changed their first didy. To achieve that end, he promised them, he intended to pound, prod, push, and hammer them to the best of their abilities, so that everyone went on to the eleventh grade with a solid understanding of mathematics and language. It did not matter if none of them went to college, mathematics and language were the cornerstones of learning; mastering algebra, geometry, Latin, and English gave them the tools to tackle anything beyond.

He expressed the same attitude toward reading and writing. He made them write large and clear. He made them spell a word until that word was second-nature. He made them read aloud as rapidly as they could, pronouncing every word distinctly, and when they spoke a word they did not know, he sent them straight to the dictionary. He made them memorize one new word every day, and he urged them to read everything they could get their hands on. He told them how he felt about books: Some were froth, lively and entertaining, fun to read and good for digestion, but like a glass of beer with a big head, all foam, no brew, your nose was tickled but your thirst wasn't quenched.

He had waited impatiently to teach the ninth-grade class; in his private estimation, they were the best group of students in his tenure. He saw the potential in Patrick Brown and Ernest Stonecifer, Lionel Maas and Edwin Showalter, Marion Dee Potts and Vera Stensrud, Walter Kelton and Harvey Marquardt. He wanted to push them so hard they had to study every night, chewing their pencils, making their chicken tracks, wrestling with the new dimensions and perceptions taking shape in their minds, the dreams as clear-cut as diamond facets, the thoughts rougher than rocks forming in time. He wanted them to ponder that seeming contradiction: Thoughts should be clear, dreams unfinished snippets in the night. He wanted them to struggle with the growing, frightening realization that they knew practically nothing about the vast bulk of knowledge in the world.

ON THE EVENING of that second day in school, William Phegley sat to supper in Heck Hanson's house, where he had boarded since coming to Cherrygrove. As he shook out his napkin, Heck asked the yearly question: "How did it go?"

"Good start."

"How many pupils this year?"

"One hundred and six."

"How do the country kids stack up?"

"Better than average bunch, one above-average mind. A girl named Vera Stensrud. She's quick and sharp, a lot like Marion Dee Potts."

"Who'll top their class, Bill?"

"Marion Dee, Patrick, this new girl Vera, Ernest if he wants to."

"Wants to?"

"You know how Ernest gobbles up everything he wants to use, and learns everything else because he has to. It's a matter of how he applies himself."

"I wonder what he wants?"

"I don't know yet, Heck, but give me this year to gain his confidence."

"You've already got it, Bill."

"Did he tell you that?"

"No, Marion Dee did."

"I thought so."

"Good guess, Bill. They've been that way ever since I can remember."

William Phegley ate with relish and resisted the temptation to tell Heck that he was going west in two years. He had already given his oral promise to become principal of a four-year high school in the sandhill town of Ophelia. He had to go; it meant a better salary and a bigger challenge. But for two more years in Cherrygrove, he would do his level best, and his best was very good. He intended to tell Heck next fall, just as he would tell Pat Brown, the lumberman, who was president of the school board, so that Pat would have plenty of time to find a new principal. William Phegley had deep respect for Pat Brown, with one reservation: If he had married a woman like Virginia Brown—God forbid!—he would never give in to her as often as Pat did. On the other hand, Pat stood fast for his son, so perhaps the judgment was too harsh; it might be that Pat enjoyed the way he lived with his wife, had discovered it was the best way to maintain a precarious balance in the most dangerous union known to man. Heck Hanson chose that moment to say, "Bill, how come you've never married?"

Heck was a mystic, the way he smiled guilelessly and popped a question that matched William Phegley's secret thoughts. He gave the truthful answer Heck deserved.

"I've never met the right woman."

"Never?"

"Honest to God, Heck. Oh, there have been some nice women, but marriage? Who wants to marry a schoolteacher?"

"How old are you, Bill?"

"Thirty-seven."

"You grew up on a farm . . ." Heck was musing, not asking a question. William Phegley had related his life story years ago: the farm boy who graduated from a small-town high school and worked two years as a hired man to save enough money to enroll at the state university. He took every odd job he could find to augment his income, and had completed three years when war broke out. He enlisted, came home in the spring of 1919, and graduated the following year. He taught in other small towns prior to Cherrygrove, while attending summer school to get his master's degree; by then he had built a rock-solid reputation as a teacher, but as a man? According to his own estimate, his life had been every bit as interesting as building a henhouse. He smiled, remembering the night he had said that, and Heck continued, ". . . now for the big question, Bill. If you met the right woman, would you consider marriage?"

William Phegley's black brows jumped in a sudden transformation of spirit that softened the severe tutorial lines of his face;

the shift in mood unmasked the laughter rarely exposed in the classroom.

"Tricky question, Heck. How can I know until I meet her, then how can I ask if she doesn't encourage me?"

"Don't try to weasel out, Bill. Would you?"

William Phegley sighed. "Good God, yes!"

"Good for you—now excuse me. Got to finish supper and be ready to go with Pat Brown and the children."

"Where to?"

"Miriam Allen's. She's got a new litter of puppies, the best ever, and Patrick's dog died last summer. You remember Shep?"

"Yes, fine dog."

"Pat got Shep from Charley Lang on Patrick's second birthday. They grew up together. Good friend of mine, old Shep. Want to come along, watch Patrick pick the pride of the litter?"

"Thanks, Heck, but I've got too much to do."

"If you're still up when I get back, I'll tell you all about it."

Two

EVERYONE IN CHERRYGROVE agreed that Martha Lang and Miriam Allen had a lot in common. They were not referring to the fact that Martha and Miriam were the youngest daughters of two old settlers; what they really meant was that the two women were plainly doomed to spinsterhood. Martha kept house for her father and, disregarding her so-called engagement to Shorty LaFollette, would go on doing what she was doing until her father died, and she died, and her memory was laid to single rest. Miriam Allen was four years younger, and not at all like Martha physically, but people persisted in saying so, persuaded no doubt by the illusion of similarity created in their minds.

Miriam was taller, leaner, and more oval-faced, and her brown hair was worn in a style that Heck Hanson's housekeeper, Mrs. Osborne, called "helter-skelter"; Miriam wore shirts, overalls, and heavy brogans, excepting those occasions she came to town, went to church on Sunday, and made shopping trips to Bent Fork. Then she wore plain-colored dresses with one of the leather belts she tooled during the winter months, a pair of low-heeled oxfords, and she brushed her hair into a semblance of order. She was scrupulously clean and she always smelled fresh, but she looked uncomfortable in dresses.

Miriam liked farming and she was better at it than most men. She was a good cook, kept her house spotless, and was equally critical of her livestock, outbuildings, and machinery. She was six-teen years old when her mother died, and Edgar Allen thanked his lucky stars she had come late because his older children were married and gone. Miriam became his strong right arm before he fully appreciated her worth; by then, she was old enough to take charge. Edgar Allen turned the home farm over to her and moved into town, not that he liked town life better, but he had a nice sense of not wanting to be underfoot, and his move told her wordlessly that he had absolute confidence in her judgment. She was twenty-one when that happened, in 1915.

She had been on the farm ever since, through the war years and the beginning of Prohibition and the false prosperity of the twenties. She made money every year, even in 1922, when many farmers lost their shirts trying to pay off high-interest war mort-gages on overpriced land. Miriam planted, harvested, and went about her business of raising the finest Poland Chinas in the county. She had a real feel for swine. She had not gone to college, but she took all the pertinent extension courses offered by the university, bought the best books on her favorite subject, and was never too proud to consult someone who knew more than she did about the science. It *was* a science; hogs were more susceptible to disease than other animals and needed a great deal of care and at-tention. Miriam was one of the first farmers to use sanitary-steel watering troughs, and it was quite a sight to watch her haul the one-hundred-gallon galvanized tank around her hog yards on a heavy angle-steel sled pulled by her big bay team. She used all the minerals recommended by the college of agriculture, and she welcomed a new worm tablet because it replaced the dangerous balling gun her father had been forced to use in earlier days. She used medicated hog oil to prevent and kill lice, and regularly boiled out her round pig-feeding pens and hog troughs. She in-stalled six-foot, twenty-five bushel automatic hog feeders, and she was faster and cleaner than most men with the improved extrac-tor. She could punch nose holes and insert copper-plated rings as fast as she pushed each hog into the clamp chute; and finally, she rendered beautiful lard and cooked hog food in one of the first high-grade boilers in the county.

Miriam rarely deviated from her daily routine, but one such event was the birth of a new litter by her fox terrier bitch, Begonia, who had to change *her* routine to nurse the puppies until she could return to the serious business of minding the hogs. Begonia was the best pig dog for miles around. Miriam had gone against established custom, but she had a theory that a small dog would be more effective with brood sows, and Begonia had proved the point. The sows obeyed her, where before her advent they often bridled at bigger dogs. It was almost as if they considered Begonia too worrisome not to obey, simply to get her out of the pens. She was fussy with piglets, and direct as a sharp nip with the stags.

On that cool September night, Miriam awaited the arrival of Pat Brown, his son Patrick, Patrick's friends, and Heck Hanson. The reason for their visit was Begonia's finest litter of puppies, whose birth coincided with the Browns' need for a new dog to take the place of Shep. Miriam was eager to greet them because, as she had told Heck Hanson earlier in the week, she had heard so many stories about Patrick's uncanny ability to pick the best puppy, or kitten, that she wanted to see if he would choose the white and black male with the exceptionally bright eyes. An hour after supper, car lights swung off the highway into the Allen lane and stopped beside the back gate. The children tumbled out, calling hello as Miriam greeted them and shook hands with Pat and Heck. Pat said drily, "Here are the Indians," and Miriam led them all into the kitchen where she spoke firmly to the fox terrier lying neck deep in puppies on a red-and-black rag rug.

"Friends, Begonia. Friends."

The children squatted in a semicircle around the rug. Patrick Brown said, "Hello, Begonia," and extended his right hand to the nape of the rug. Begonia touched it with her shoe-button nose and wiggled her stub tail, and the other children chorused ever so softly, "Hello, Begonia," and received a quiet whine that signified Begonia was much taken with these polite visitors. Miriam brought the Coleman from the kitchen table to provide more light, and they all watched Patrick squat motionless for thirty seconds before putting a forefinger on the head of the white and black puppy with the bright eyes. He said, "This one, please," and smiled up at Miriam. The other children immediately began rubbing Begonia's ears while the puppies squirmed over one another and urinated on the rug in excitement at so many strange smells. Marion Dee lifted the bright-eyed puppy against her cheek. "What are you going to name him, Patrick?"

"Mickey."

"He looks like a Mickey," Miriam said. "Do you think so, Pat?"

"Eyes, ears, tail and all. When can we get him, Miriam?"

"What about a week from tonight?"

"Fine and dandy."

"Well," Miriam said, "now that that's settled, who's for a cookie?" and turned to bring the jar from the pantry. While the children ate sugar cookies and sneaked crumbs to Begonia, Miriam asked Heck how many pupils were in school that year.

"Hundred and six."

"How many in high school?"

"Twenty-five."

Miriam whistled soundlessly. "That'll keep Mr. Phegley busy."

"As a beaver." Heck cocked his head. "Is that rain?"

"Sure is," Pat Brown said. "Early this year. We better make tracks."

Miriam saw them off and returned to the house. Through the evening, redding up, then reading, she rejoiced at the coming of rain. The smell crept into the house and told her nose it was wet outside with the sweet odor of fall rain on leaves and grass and bare earth, silent rain falling out of a slate gray sky onto the roof, into the eave troughs, down the drainpipes into the cistern, carrying a few leaves that would disintegrate and eventually rise up through the pump, to be strained out before the amber-colored water was used to wash her hair and clothing. Once a mouse died in the cistern and the smell lingered for days before fading into a dusty, dry scent that vanished with the first frost.

Undressing, getting into bed and turning out the light, Miriam could not hear the rain, absorbed by the shingles above her head. She curled up in a loose, warm knot, and later in the night felt Begonia jump lightly on the bed, give her a soft sniff, and then jump down again, to return to her puppies on the thick rug beside the stove.

Three

HECK HANSON COULD never understand why some people amassed great piles of trivia. They saved Gladstone buckles and horseshoe nails years after the grip was lost and the team sold, and they seemed to spend their happiest moments picking over those worthless treasures, fondling an old perfume bottle, rubbing the surface of a broken breadboard, thinking whatever it was their minds hugged in private adoration. Heck fought a silent pitch-and-toss war with his housekeeper, who saved everything she got her hands on. He was out in the barn emptying barrels on the sly while she filled boxes in the basement, so that a rough balance was maintained, with the scales tipped slightly in her favor.

"She's younger," Heck told William Phegley after dinner on Thanksgiving Day. "She'll outlast me."

"Why does she do it?"

Heck chuckled. "I finally decided it comes down to the simple act of having the freedom to dream."

"Simple act!"

"I know it isn't simple," Heck said, "but assume you live in a country rich enough to let its dreamers dream without producing anything worth selling. That nation is rich beyond avarice."

"Now you are dreaming, Heck."

"Humor me."

"If you'll humor me."

"Shoot."

"The day school started, before you went out to Miriam Allen's that night, you asked me why I never married."

Heck nodded. "And being honest, you admitted you had never met the right woman."

"In line with that," William Phegley went on, "I was talking with Pat Brown after school yesterday, and out of a clear blue sky he asked if I liked hogs. I told him I could take them or leave them, and then he asked how well I knew Edgar Allen. I told him pretty well, Edgar's your friend and neighbor, we say hello almost every day. Next thing I knew, Pat was asking me how well I knew Miriam Allen, and I said to say hello."

"Good God!" Heck said. "You teach here eight years and don't know Miriam better than that?"

"Remember, I'm gone summers."

"That's no excuse—do you want to know her better?"

"Why do you think I'm pumping you? The way Pat went on talking about her, she sounds like an independent human being."

"There's no such animal, but she comes close."

"Where does she miss?"

"Where so many people do, her pride and joy."

"Hogs?"

"What a pleasure to philosophize with you, Bill. You catch on so fast! Yes, hogs. She's so good with them, she forgets to keep them in balance with the rest of her life."

"Maybe she never had a fair crack at whatever it is you call 'the rest of her life.'"

"She didn't," Heck said, "and by the time she had the chance, she was weighed down with so much responsibility and common sense, she couldn't recognize what she'd missed. I used to kid her about it when she was young—that was before you came—and still had time to change. She'd sit here, where you're sitting, drinking my coffee, smiling and nodding, agreeing with me about things she would never do, much less try, until I felt like putting her over my knee and spanking a little fun into her. That's what she's missed, Bill, a lot of the fun of living. That's why Pat Brown mentioned her. He must believe you two could hit it off."

"Oh come on, Heck!"

"No, you come on, Bill! Look at yourself, you've missed a lot of fun too. She's got hogs, you've got school."

"Not much common ground, Heck."

"More than meets the eye. You like children, she does too."

"She does?"

"Age is no barrier to friendship. All your prize ninth-graders are her good friends. Do you think she'd give Patrick Brown her best puppy if she didn't trust him? And while we're on the subject, did Pat mention an indoor basketball court to you yesterday?"

"No."

"Wise man, didn't want to cloud your mind with other issues. But I'm sure you know how much Patrick and his friends would love to have one, where they can practice without mittens and be shed of shoveling snow off that outdoor court all winter long. Well, in recognition of their entering high school, Pat, Charley Lang, and yours truly are going to play Santa Claus."

"Where?"

"The dance pavilion," Heck said. "Backboards can go above the stage and over the vestibule entrance. Charley is paying for the backboards, Pat donates the baskets and nets, I'm buying a new indoor basketball. The pavilion will be open on Wednesday nights and Sunday afternoons, on the condition they wear tennis shoes, take care of the fires, and sweep up afterward. You are invited, whenever you can find time."

William Phegley gave his friend a long, searching look. "I don't see it, but there's got to be a catch."

"Of course there is," Heck said complacently. "There's no free lunch."

THE CHILDREN HELD their first indoor basketball practice on Wednesday, New Year's Day, and found it blissful to play without coats, caps, and mittens. As time passed, they sharpened their jumping, passing, dribbling, shooting and—perhaps most important—using their peripheral vision so that one player guarding another was not tipped off to the next move by head or eye shift. Patrick and Ernest played the guards, Marion Dee was center, with Edwin and Lionel at the forwards. Pat Brown's yardman, Pete Olson, flanked by Hurryup Maas and Johnny Showalter, played the defense, and that was the weak spot. They could never muster two full teams.

On the first Sunday afternoon in February, Shorty LaFollette tramped into the pavilion, took off his coat and cap, kicked off his overshoes, and stood before them in an ancient gray sweatsuit and dirt-stained tennis shoes. Shorty had never mentioned playing basketball before coming to Cherrygrove, but he had played, and he bolstered the defense needed to test their growing skills.

A week later, Marion Dee invited Miriam Allen to come over after Sunday dinner with her father. Miriam had never played basketball but she put on a pair of tennis shoes and joined the defense where she surprised everyone with her agility. Marion Dee just grinned like a Cheshire cat; she had known all along that Miriam was not the bulky woman people thought she was under her loose, shapeless clothes.

They got a bigger surprise on Wednesday night when William Phegley came through the front door with Pete Olson and Shorty LaFollette, wearing a faded blue sweatsuit and real Converse basketball shoes, red stocking cap on his black head, blue checkered bandanna tied around his neck. He shook hands with Miriam Allen, smiled at his pupils, and said, "Where do you want me?"

Marion Dee spoke right up. "You're tallest, Mr. Phegley. Take center."

The addition of William Phegley gave them a full team on defense. Now they could play practice games and learn much faster from actual experience. William Phegley was five feet, ten inches tall, but did not use his height unfairly. He always passed the ball to Hurryup and Johnny, and was careful not to rebound too much. When they took time out to catch their breath, he sat beside the cloakroom stove with Miriam Allen and Marion Dee, rubbing Begonia's ears and helping Miriam study the rule book. They were very polite to each other, and seemed to get along just fine.

On the last Sunday afternoon in February, Miriam brought two dark-complected men who turned out to be identical twins, Ross and Roy Royce. They had recently bought the old Anderson place and become Miriam's new neighbors to the west. They got out of their caps, coats, and overshoes, and stood in worn basketball shoes and patched yellow sweatsuits with the name OPHELIA on their backs. They watched for ten minutes before Pete Olson motioned them to take over the defensive forward positions from Hurryup and Johnny, and then, for the first time, Patrick and Ernest had their hands full. The Royce twins gave no quarter, guarded like mustard plasters, and showed a bewildering variety of offensive moves. That afternoon marked the date on which they began playing basketball the way the game was meant to be played.

During rest periods, Ross Royce showed them how to stand, back to the basket, fake with one shoulder, half turn, and make a quick backhand pass to a teammate cutting for the basket. The fake had to be convincing enough to pull the guard to that side, giving you floor space to make the backhand pass; then, off a side or center post, Roy Royce showed them how to come in high on the foul line and work what he called a give, and go with either guard, on the guard's signal. Roy Royce was the best long shot they had ever seen. He could stand anywhere along the imaginary curved line that touched the top of the foul circle and consistently make seven out of ten, this feat accomplished under the handicap of ceiling rafters that made regular arched shots impossible. Roy just lowered his arc and used the backboard.

Pete Olson named Wednesday night, March eighteenth, as the last practice of the winter. The pavilion was warm with fires and good fellowship that night, and they played to a small gallery for the first time. Both teams came to the center jump circle, Pat Brown threw up the ball, Patrick got the tip from Ross Royce, and they were off with youthful gasps and older grunts, passing and dribbling and shooting, tennis shoes whacking the floor, ball bang-ing hardwood and backboards and iron hoops, swishing through the nets, lifting dust in the glare of the bare lightbulbs. Martha Lang came with Shorty LaFollette and Miriam, carrying a big lunch basket filled with cookies, mugs, and a thermos jug of hot chocolate. After the last shot, they gathered around the stove in the lunch counter corner, ate cookies and drank hot chocolate and talked about the winter past and the summer yet to come.

"Well," Pat Brown said, "who wants a ride home?"

The children chorused, "I do!" and the front door banged open, wind blew Bob Showalter inside and propelled him across the dance floor toward the lunch counter with such an air of gravity that everybody was prepared for the worst before he opened his mouth. Edwin said, "What's the matter, Pa?" and Bob Showalter coughed to steady his voice.

"I'm sorry to break up the game, Edwin, but you and Johnny better get dressed and come with me. Your grandfather has passed away."

Four

FOLLOWING THE SERVICES at the cemetery, William Phegley sat at his desk and remembered the faces ringing the grave: old faces, contemporaries of Ed Showalter, sharers of fifty years of common yesterdays. William Phegley asked himself, What is yesterday? So many places, too many faces, two pounds of words, one quart of dreams, life the weight of feathers? You put the question to today and it promises an answer no later than tomorrow, but tomorrow becomes yesterday and time moves on, promising eternity, leaving questions. Who is God? What is a vacuum? What did Socrates do when he wasn't teaching? Where did old Roman legionnaires go to die? What variety of apple hit Newton on the head? Why did men wage war, did Lily Langtry really use Pears Soap, how stands the Union? You asked, you searched for truth and gathered shadows, ran them through your mind and let them go. Time moved on, passing through you, leading you forward even as you fell back, renewing and dying in the same breath, the same unanswered wonder.

William Phegley put on his coat and went downstairs, out of the silent schoolhouse into heatless spring sunshine; pillar of the community, unshaken by natural or human circumstances, taking the two-block walk to his rooms. The outer shell strolled briskly, the inner self quaked like a bowl of jelly, aware of death's specter, conscious of spring's birth for the first time in years. He came to

Heck Hanson's front porch, put his right foot on the bottom step, and halted—he had forgotten the ninth grade Latin test papers. If he retraced his steps, all the town would know he had spring fever.

Good Lord! he thought. What's wrong with me?

He knew, and he could find no handle capable of jacking up his spirits. He sat down to supper with Heck, chewed methodically through Mrs. Osborne's roast beef, mashed potatoes, brown gravy, coleslaw, peas, and apple pie, folded his napkin, and followed Heck into the living room. Heck lit his after-supper cigar and sank into his aged black leather chair beside the low table stacked with newspapers, magazines, and books, through which his left hand would soon drift and burrow like a mole. Heck blew smoke and stared through the cloud.

"Sad day."

William Phegley nodded. "He was well liked."

"Was he?"

"You know what I mean, Heck."

"Bill, there's an old saying that goes 'I never met a man I didn't like.' I've always taken that with a bushel of salt, especially since Will Rogers said it publicly, because he's seen enough of his fellow man to know he should have said 'I finally met a man I like.' To the best of my arithmetic, if I like one man in every ten I meet, I'm ahead of the hounds. As for women, I've always believed that the best time to meet them is at the age of ten. I have enjoyed great success, and furthered my education, not to mention my personal pleasure, in having met and gotten to know several young ladies of age ten, and in two cases, continued our friendship until they reached womanhood, married, and had children of their own. In both cases, my original assessment turned out favorably, and in one instance, the woman improved on the child she had been. Off that evidence, I would say there is more chance of meeting a woman I like than a man, so what's this I hear about Miriam Allen being stuck on you?"

William Phegley's jaw dropped in wonder and admiration. The way Heck soothed his victim before delivering the knockout punch was an ever-recurring delight, even for the victim. He began, "I don't know about her—"

"What about you?"

"I—"

"You like her?"

"I do, but we haven't had much chance to get acquainted."

"Too crowded at basketball practice?"

"Yes."

"Then put on your best bib and tucker and pay her a visit."

William Phegley hoped he could explain why he hesitated. Heck smiled encouragement. "Well?"

"Heck, it wouldn't be fair to her."

"Why not?"

"Because I'd be seeing her under false pretenses."

"Just because next year is your last year here?"

William Phegley swallowed shocked surprise. "How the hell did you find that out?"

"I wasn't prying, Bill. Jim Lang buys yearlings from Burt Miller every spring. Burt's ranch is south of Ophelia, and his brother, as you know, is president of the Ophelia school board. He told Burt they considered themselves lucky to get you. Burt mentioned it to Jim Lang, Jim naturally told Pat Brown, and Pat told me."

William Phegley shook his head in resignation. "I should have known."

"Sure you should, but that's not important. What is, is you not wanting to be unfair to Miriam Allen. Why don't you give it a try, and if things start to work out, tell her all about your future plans, see what she says. You might as well—you're under a handicap anyway."

"What handicap?"

"Her farm."

William Phegley snapped his fingers. "My God, what's the matter with me! Every bachelor in this neck of the woods must set his cap for that farm."

"They do."

"Well, the hell with the farm!"

"I understand that too, Bill."

"Heck, is there anything you don't understand?"

"Yes, but I've never told a living soul."

"Excuse me, I didn't mean to pry." William Phegley rose and went to the hall door. "Thanks, Heck."

"Hold on, it's past time I told somebody, before I take the secret to my grave."

"Are you joking?"

"Never more serious," Heck said, smiling through his cigar smoke. "What I don't understand, and probably never will, is why we humans put blinders on horses."

"Why, to keep them from—"

"Whoa! Think first, speak later. Why do we, the whole damn human race, put blinders on horses when we wear them ourselves, day and night? Wouldn't you think we'd want a good, clear look to the right, to the left, and straight ahead, during our own ride through life? Goodnight, Bill. Have Mrs. Osborne press your gray jacket."

IT TOOK WILLIAM Phegley a week to get up his Dutch courage. On the following Saturday he bathed and shaved, put on his gray flannel trousers, a blue-checked cotton flannel shirt, maroon knit tie, black oxfords, and his freshly pressed gray tweed jacket with the scuffed leather elbow patches, and drove west from town as though heading for Bent Fork. Four miles down the road, he turned into the Allen lane and entered the yard at one o'clock in the afternoon. Miriam Allen appeared in her kitchen doorway, shaded her eyes, and blushed in pink surprise, even as she smiled a welcome.

"Hello, Mr. Phegley."

"Hello, Miriam." *Mister* Phegley opened the gate and bent down to rub the fox terrier's ears. "Hello, Begonia."

"She likes you."

"Probably wonders if I brought the basketball." He would never forget how Begonia sat on the aisle bench beside Miriam's neatly folded coat, cap, and muffler, and watched the action with her bright black eyes. "How are you?"

"Just fine, and you?"

"Fine, thanks." Having exhausted the state of their health, William Phegley looked around the farmyard. "I decided to take you up on your invitation and drive out. Have you got time to show me around?"

Miriam tried to remember when she had invited him, but it did not matter, she was so glad to see him. She said, "Lots of time," and led the way across the yard to the big hog shed south of the barn on the shelf of ground that sloped away toward the creek in the pasture bottom. William Phegley took his farmer's eye out of cold storage and studied the layout: deep loess soil with a touch of sand from the veins that paralleled the Bent Fork River four miles to the west, the sand advertising the presence of coarse gravel thirty to sixty feet beneath the surface, making for excellent drainage conditions. The outbuildings were in first-class shape, the machinery was under a roof, and the interior of the big hog shed was as clean and odor-free as could possibly be. He looked at the hogs, and stopped in the barn to see the big bay team, before returning to the house where Miriam made tea and cut a chocolate cake. William Phegley smiled.

"Heck told me what to expect."

"What's that?"

"You're the best farmer out here."

Miriam blushed. "Heck said that?"

"He did."

"I wish he'd tell Pa."

"Why?"

"Sometimes Pa takes me for granted."

William Phegley shook his head. "I don't think so."

"You don't know Pa that well."

"I could argue the point, but Heck does."

Miriam gave him a level stare. "Is that why you drove out?"

"No, and don't get the wrong idea. It's not because I like farming. I don't."

"I think you mean that."

"I do."

"Then why?"

"Because I liked you the minute we got to doing more than saying hello," William Phegley said bluntly, "and I'd like to know you better. Do you mind?"

Miriam's reply was equally direct. "No."

"There's just one thing. My first name is William. Call me Bill, will you?"

"Glad to," Miriam said, and smiled. "I know why they call you Mister."

William Phegley nodded. "I sometimes wonder where that custom started."

"I don't know," Miriam said, "but we were doing it when I was in school. That was Mr. Burns, then he left and the one named Mr. Kadelka came, did you meet him when you took over?"

"No, but I knew his cousin Joe. We were at the university together. They're from the Howells country."

"Bohemian?"

"One hundred percent," William Phegley said. "Biggest men and women you ever saw. You're tall for our generation, but those Bohemian girls must run five-five on the average."

"Have another piece of cake?"

"Thank you."

Eating cake, drinking tea, they discovered that talking together was effortless because they had so much mutual experience to draw on. They began discussing his ninth-grade class, a subject that occupied them for more than an hour when William Phegley learned that Miriam knew a great deal about every child in the class, knowledge that went far beyond playing basketball twice a week. He asked if she knew much about Vera Stensrud, who had gotten over her initial shyness to become one of his best students. Miriam explained that Vera's parents grew up nearer Slayton in what was originally called Little Sweden. Mrs. Stensrud's maiden name was Nordstrum and she was just as good-looking as her daughter. Vera's father was an average farmer trying to make a living on indifferent land inclined to clay streaks along the south slopes. Being an only child, Vera was trying to take the place of a son for her father, but in turn, he was not a man to take advantage, so Vera had never been forced into doing anything she did not volunteer—was that what he wanted to know?

William Phegley lied gracefully. "It helps a lot."

Miriam understood his predicament; it was difficult to talk about sex at any time, let alone during their first serious conversation. She said, "But not enough?"

"Not quite."

"What is it?"

"There's something about Vera that bothers me."

"I know."

"Are you sure you do?"

"I'm sure," Miriam said. "It's natural at her age."

William Phegley breathed a sigh of relief. Miriam *did* understand. Now was his chance to learn more about the girl, so that, should the occasion arise, he might be able to help her.

"What was Mrs. Stensrud like at Vera's age?"

"The same way—" Miriam compounded her indirectness in order to make William Phegley feel more at ease while they spoke ambiguously. "But I was too. It's a funny feeling that gets into you around fourteen or fifteen, at least it did to me, and you know what it is but you don't know how to handle it. Vera's lucky to be in a small school. If there were more girls, they'd resent her for growing up faster."

"That's it," William Phegley said. "She's clean and neat, she wears nice dresses, but she's got that look that seems to say she'd rather be wearing a pair of overalls."

"I ought to know."

"I'm sorry, I didn't mean—"

"I know you didn't," Miriam said, "but the truth never hurt anybody. I sit out here weeks at a time and forget about dresses.

Once I tried on a pair of high-heeled shoes and nearly broke my ankles."

William Phegley changed the subject, not that Miriam seemed ashamed to be caught in a pair of overalls, but there were so many things he suddenly wanted to talk over with her that he was afraid they'd never be able to pour everything out on the table between them. It was five o'clock before he realized how late it was and made himself say good afternoon, and driving back to town, he wondered where the time had gone.

Five

WILLIAM PHEGLEY MADE his annual place-name speech on Thursday, May twenty-first, the day before school closed for the summer.

"Arab," he began. "Flagstaff, Festus, Los Gatos, Durango, Beacon Falls, Dover, Tarpon Springs, Fair Oaks, Blackfoot, Du Quoin, Wabash, Coon Rapids, Clay Center, Bardstown—was it named for Shakespeare or a wheelwright named Bard?—New Iberia, Cape Porpoise, Frostburg, Ipswich, Bad Axe, Sleepy Eye, Yazoo City, Boonville . . ." He always named one town in each state, in alphabetical order of states, and every year he named new towns. ". . . Havre, Mora, Great Neck, Mount Airy, Devils Lake, Kenton, Kingfisher—is that for a bird or a bad man?—Tillamook, Conshohocken, Woonsocket, Sumter, Spearfish, Lebanon, Ranger, Heber, Snohomish, White Sulphur Springs, Baraboo, Thermopolis."

He turned to the blackboard and wrote names in six-inch letters: Broken Bow, Scottsbluff, Sundance, Cody, Cutbank, Mobridge, Belle Fourche. "Names," he said, with a sweep of his chalk, "spoken every day by people who never once wonder where they came from, what they mean. Do you know the meaning of Mobridge, Broken Bow, Belle Fourche? Come closer home. How about Burnside, Bent Fork, Blackbird County, Buckhorn, Little Sweden? Are you curious enough to look up the names and learn

94

their meaning? Can you name the creeks and rivers and lakes and swamps all across our country? Can you name the deserts and forests and mountains? Bring me some of those names next September, tell me how they came to be, what they mean to you. Pikes Peak, Rainier, Peedee, Bull Run, Wasatch, Mohave, Black Water, Olympic, Siberia. Names! How they do run on!"

On the following afternoon, a fine May Saturday filled with spring fever, William Phegley started his now regular drive to Bent Fork; as was equally regular, he never arrived. Four miles west of town, he turned into the Allen lane and parked beside the backyard gate, where Miriam greeted him with a kiss and led him up the walk into the house; taking off his cap, William Phegley knelt down and gave Begonia a good welcome scratching at the base of her fine ears. He took a cup of coffee from Miriam and warmed his hands while his heart touched the woman he had come to love. He wondered again how it could have happened in two short, joyous months, and now that school was out, how he could leave her for the summer. To ease that fresh worry, he told her about his place-name speech, and watched her eyes light up as she cast through personal memory for examples of their American birthright.

"Bill, I've got one for you."

"What?"

"Dinky Creek."

"Where?"

"It runs into the Missouri, west of the Indian burial grounds on the chalk bluffs. Now tell me what it was named for."

"A small stream."

"No."

"A brook, one yard wide and one-inch deep."

"You're getting cold."

William Phegley raised his arms in mock surrender. "I give up."

Miriam laughed gleefully. "After a man named Dinky."

"No!"

"Yes, his name was Gus Dinky, he farmed up there around 1900. My father knew him."

William Phegley put his coffee cup on the table and took her in his arms. They stood for a long time, holding each other firmly in silent enjoyment of what could be. He finally broke their thrall, stepped back, and found a passable smile.

"Well, summer's here."

"When do you leave?"

"I'll have to go Monday. I promised my brother, he needs the help, but—oh, hell!"

"Cheer up, it's only three months."

"What makes you so cheerful, changed your mind since we talked last Saturday?"

Miriam shook her head. William Phegley had asked her if she would marry him at the end of the 1932 school year and move with him to Ophelia. He had not tendered the proposal in the form of an ultimatum, nor had he the slightest wish to do so, but it was something they had to discuss fairly. Miriam had spent most of that afternoon trying to explain—perhaps mostly to herself— why she could not leave her father alone in town, and was not sure she had the strength to break away from the farm. William Phegley understood. They loved each other, and they were not children. He had to go, and she had solid, lifelong reasons for staying. The way it looked, they decided, they should respect each other's responsibilities until the spring of 1932; surely another year was more than enough time to reach a mutual decision. Meanwhile, Miriam voiced a daring thought that had entered her mind during the week.

"Bill, should we go to bed?"

"I want to," William Phegley said. "Good Lord, yes, but that's no solution."

"I know, but I thought I ought to ask."

"I'm glad you did. Does it make you feel better?"

"No."

"Me neither. Maybe we ought to go in and take batting practice with Patrick and Ernest."

Miriam laughed and leaned her head against his shoulder. He was close to being one of a kind in their day and age. He came from a farm where the finest reading a boy could find was on tin can labels, and he had never satisfied his appetite for words that exploded the wonderful pictures of unknown life in his mind. He read to learn, and he read to feel the emotions that burst from the characters who raced across the pages of Dickens and Sterne and Swift and Bunyan, yes, even the gray-brown pulp pages of *Street and Smith* and *Argosy*, and lesser lights that provided no more than a candle's flame in the ignorant darkness. They all illuminated some part of living; and he wanted to feel that part in eye, on skin, between the fingers of his consciousness. Miriam felt it when she began to know him and responded so enthusiastically that she frightened her own sense of humor. William Phegley made her feel the wonder of her own birth. No small wonder people fell in love.

Six

SUMMER BLOOMED. MIRIAM tried to recapture her customary flow of life, but the glow of satisfaction had faded from early summer's warmth, the growth of piglets, and the anticipation of expecting William Phegley every Saturday afternoon to pass what had become the finest hours of her waking existence. How could she fill the terrible emptiness created by his departure? In desperation, she turned to the friend who always soothed her. She drove into town, sat in Martha Lang's big kitchen, looked out the bay window toward the roof of Shorty LaFollette's house showing gray-shingled through the green leaves, and talked about the riches they shared: cooking, baking, sewing, the price of corn, oats, cattle, hogs—good God! when they got down to brass tacks and wanted to keep a spirited conversation going, there was no end to everything they could discuss. How in the world had they managed to nurture, and share, so many valuable thoughts and emotions? Better not raise the specter of love. Miriam's was far to the south, and Martha's was where Shorty would always be, two blocks away in the implement shop. They sat drinking tea, eating Martha's delicious cookies, blinking at the flash of a passing blue jay, iridescent for a split second in the sunlight. Miriam felt the ghost of all the spinsters who had lived and died in Cherrygrove, looking down or up, as their case might be, and speaking purse-lipped, "Stop the reverie, you both know how it will turn out."

"No!" Miriam said aloud.

"Eh?"

"Sorry, Martha. I was daydreaming."

"Me too."

"You?"

Martha's seldom exposed sense of humor surfaced for a brief, ironic smile. "Is it against the law for me?"

"Oh no! I didn't mean that."

"I know you didn't—will Mr. Phegley be gone all summer?"

"I think so."

"He's a good man." Martha changed the subject: "Got some news for you."

"What?"

"Pa had Jim buy the gas station yesterday."

The gas station across the street from the lumberyard had been opened by Oscar Tyson in 1922. When demand warranted it, he bought a truck to deliver tractor fuel and gas to the farmers, and he worked long and hard to build up his business. In the process he erected a storage tank, sheds, and grease pit, and added an ever-expanding line of accessories, but his most valuable acquisition was his hired man. Franklin Krug was one of those quiet, capable men who could do everything around a small-town place of business; like Shorty LaFollette, he was absolutely trustworthy. As time passed, Oscar Tyson was able to indulge his passion for hunting and fishing, secure in the knowledge that Franklin was taking care of everything. Oscar did not figure on such extenuating circumstances as the market crash, drouth, and the Depression.

Miriam compressed his tragedy in two words: "Going broke?"

"He told Jim he just couldn't make it."

"Did Franklin refuse the manager's job?"

Martha smiled. "You know Franklin, he wants no part of being boss. But he agreed to be acting manager until Jim finds a good man. Jim made him take ten dollars a month more salary."

"I'll bet he tried to turn it down."

"He did. He tried to convince Jim he didn't deserve a raise because how could he deliver tractor fuel and run the station at the same time?"

"How did Jim get around that argument?"

"He told Franklin to lock the front door and make the deliveries, and during the summers Jim could hire a good boy to help out."

Now where would Jim Lang find a boy who could pump gas, fill radiators, change oil, grease, fix flats, put on chains, and handle the simple bookkeeping system? Miriam knew.

"Ernest Stonecifer."

"I guessed too," Martha said. "Jim hired him this morning, he started work this afternoon."

Ever since Jim Lang married Ernest's oldest sister, Charley Lang had watched Ernest grow and liked what he saw. What Charley Lang had really done, although he would never admit it, was have Jim buy the gas station with an eye toward the possible future of a fourteen-year-old boy. There had to be a place in heaven for a man like that.

SUMMER DIED. WILLIAM Phegley returned from a hard three months of work on his brother's farm, greeted his fledgling ninth-graders, built fresh fires of resolution beneath his tenth-graders, and once more drove west on Saturday afternoons. And Miriam, again at peace with self, if not with unresolved decision, welcomed him. Life renewed itself, the air cooled, leaves began turning, the world was in a miserable state. One moment they dawdled in September, then the next, Christmas had passed and changes were occurring. William Phegley watched his tenth-graders and knew the boys had become painfully conscious of the female species—only girls by the most liberal stretch of imagination, but no less complete anatomically than older women of twenty.

Not that the boys had become selective in their preference of breasts, hips, legs, and faces, they still lumped all features into a general shape, but that shape was beginning to send the first strange sensations coursing through their bodies. It was a simple, natural way to grow into sex. They already understood the business of creation; at least, they knew how it was done, but now they began to feel the impulses that triggered the act, and sense intuitively that it could only be fully appreciated through firsthand experience. William Phegley wondered if the boys realized that Vera Stensrud was the prime cause of their awakening.

Whatever it was that Vera had, it was felt by everybody in the high school room. The other girls seemed to band together like a herd of young heifers trying to protect themselves from a female wolf. Vera's emanations were innocent on her part, but felt strongly by the boys. William Phegley wished he could ask if Vera gave them all the same feeling. He knew they wanted to confide in one another, but for the first time were too self-conscious to open their mouths. One night after supper, he posed the riddle to Heck.

"Do you remember yourself?" Heck countered.

"Too damned well!"

"Were you embarrassed?"

"Ignorant, confused, *and* embarrassed."

"Did you think of asking your father?"

"Heck, you know we didn't do that."

"Do you think it's different now?"

"I hoped so."

"Hoped in vain."

William Phegley nodded rueful agreement. "Well, they may be looking for answers, but they're not turning into sex maniacs."

"Not yet," Heck said. "They've got too many important things to do. Baseball, basketball, swimming, hunting, fishing, everything that makes life worthwhile. They're still children, and we've still got enough sense to treat them like children."

"To use the fancy word, they are protected by our mores."

"Are they now?"

William Phegley smiled humorlessly. "Country, flag, family, church—"

"—school, Ladies Aid, Daughters of this, Mothers of that, Sons of God-knows-what—"

"—hand in glove with forebearance, chastity, denial—"

"—not to mention prejudice, hypocrisy, bigotry, and the healthy fear of getting the girl with child. Nothing unusual in our bag of sticks, Bill. All of them are hard at work all the time on all of us. Has Miriam made up her mind?"

"Not yet."

"Did you set her a deadline?"

"You know better than that."

"She needs time, Bill."

"I know it. Her father, the farm—"

"Life," Heck corrected gently. "Her life. We're all to blame, we can also take all the credit. We shaped her, we blessed her strengths and babied her weaknesses, gave her the reason for growing, for being, for living—for too damned much! That's the trouble, growing up in a place like this. You know everybody, you understand everything, and when you stay too long, you get scared to death just thinking of going out into the big, wide world. Want to play some chess?"

ONE DARK, FURIOUS day toward the end of February, William Phegley sat alone in the high school room at five in the afternoon, looking through the frost-rimed windows at the town. Did he like it best in spring, summer, fall, or now, when snow covered all the scars and warts? Trouble was, snow could not hide the way economic conditions were worsening; it was only a matter of months until the town would be unable to handle its own human problems. Things were coming down to time and money; there was little leeway left, and money was so short that quite a few people had already gone flat broke. That had never happened before in William Phegley's lifetime, and that night after supper, Heck admitted that things were going to get worse. William Phegley asked, "In what way?"

"Every way. Do you know Pat Brown and Bob Showalter are the only ones still extending credit?"

"I guessed."

"Coal, tar paper, nails, that sort of thing. You can't let people freeze. Drafts are awful on babies and children. And food, they've got to eat. But it's dangerous walking that credit line. You don't dare let yourself get softhearted, or you'll go under—do you know that Charley Lang has failed considerably?"

"Yes, Martha told Miriam."

Miriam had passed along the news that Charley Lang was slower walking from the breakfast table to his office room, settling back in his chair, opening the morning *World-Herald*. He had gotten thinner and grayer and his thoughts were slower. He had taken to prefacing occasional remarks with words of unpredictable direction, such as telling Shorty LaFollette how thick the rabbits were in the late eighties before asking if anybody in town was going hungry. Heck nodded glumly.

"It's arrangement time."

"Eh?"

"Every time Martha calls a number, whoever is on the switchboard—Mrs. Potts or Stella—answers, 'Number please, how's your father, Martha?' Arrangement time! People call the undertaker about arrangements. They call the county commissioner to get the road to the cemetery plowed out. Mrs. Potts and Stella know that Charley Lang is slipping, they know that all the old-timers, including me, are wearing out. It gets so they hate to answer certain numbers. Death in any season hurts the living, but in winter? Worst of all. That's why Mrs. Potts sounds so short-tempered, bites off her words when she plugs in and snarls, 'Numburr please!' until the caller thinks 'What's got into the old crosspatch today?' Life's got into her. That's winter talking."

Yes, William Phegley thought, and winter hit the children too. Growing fast in body and mind, full of energy and new ideas, trapped in winter's web. They practiced basketball on Wednesday evenings; on other, clear nights they skated on the pond behind the blacksmith shop, racing through an hour of crack-the-whip and figure-eights before going home to study. He could see them all: Ernest at the Potts's dining-room table with Marion Dee, while Mrs. Potts tended the switchboard and Sam fiddled with whatever mechanical device he had on the workbench in the shop off the kitchen. Patrick studied alone in his upstairs room, but Edwin Showalter had to suffer Johnny. Lionel Maas had no choice about sharing their kitchen table with Hurryup, and Vera Stensrud sat alone at the rolltop desk in her grandparents' bungalow. Their heads were bent over Latin and geometry, English and history, lost in the world of words and deeds and figures that, for a brief time, pulled their minds from the grim world outside their door.

THE LITTLE KIDS in the primary room sang "March winds bring April showers, April showers bring May flowers," and the magic never failed. Long underwear began to feel hot, and every industrious woman in town responded to the romantic urge of spring by announcing that housecleaning would commence on such-and-such a date. The children appreciated the return of rain and flowers, but spring to them meant carpet beaters, brooms, Bon Ami, soap, and the annual resurrection of a mania for cleanliness. By the time everything was washed, wiped, dusted, and oiled, all the gardens were planted, all the fields were sowed, and school was coming to a close.

Heck invited Miriam and her father to supper on the night before graduation. Edgar Allen had come through the winter in better shape than he expected. He sat facing William Phegley, seeing him as a man, not a principal, for the first time in their long, casual acquaintance. Evidently he liked what he saw. He could be as offhanded about the past as Charley Lang or Heck or the late Patrick Brown, Pat's father and young Patrick's grandfather; but caught in the right mood, prompted by people he trusted, he would speak with a kind of quiet, awkward eloquence. Heck got him talking about the brutal business of breaking virgin buffalo sod with plows made of inferior iron, a job that took good horses and strong backs, plus the will to work from dawn past dark. William Phegley's father and uncles had experienced the same brutal work in the southeast corner of the state, and he agreed with Edgar Allen that the only real change in method from those unlamented years were better plows and bigger horses. They talked their way from plows to seed corn to the merits of cookstoves; from the year Edgar Allen put in the first septic tank system and indoor bathroom in western Blackbird County, to the first washing machine with a dependable gas engine, one of the truly great improvements on the farm. "That washing machine," Edgar Allen said, "and the separator. Best things ever happened for women."

"I agree," William Phegley said. "I hate washboards. I mean, I *really* hate them!"

Edgar Allen gave him a small, warm smile and looked at Heck. Something wordless passed between them, that silent language the old men spoke without gesture or apparent shade of emotion. After supper, Miriam left her father and Heck nicely settled in the living room, and went out on the front porch with William Phegley. He could feel the strong pull of the past working inside her; if Edgar Allen had been a selfish, devious man, William Phegley might have suspected him of verbal *and* silent sabotage.

"Don't be late tomorrow," he said. "I'll save you a seat."

"Don't worry," Miriam said. "I'll be there."

She would not miss the graduation of her young friends for anything. What she really wanted to do was tell William Phegley that she had not come any nearer a decision than she'd been last fall. She had tried, oh God! how she had tried, but she was still on the fence. Her father looked fine tonight, but he was drawing toward the end of his life, and the thought of being a hundred miles to the west on the day or night he died, unable to get there in time to hold his hand and wish him Godspeed, was too much to bear. And there was the farm, and the hogs, and the bay team, and all the years of her life. She shivered in the pleasant May night, and William Phegley understood. He turned and gave her a hug and kissed her, right out there on the front porch in plain sight of all the town.

"Don't worry," he said. "We'll work it out."

Miriam felt the same strong pull of past and present during the simple graduation exercises held the following afternoon. She sat with parents and friends in the back of the high school room, and watched William Phegley present the report cards and certificates; by that time everyone knew she was not going to Ophelia with him. However he felt, he did not show it as he shook hands with his pupils and wished them good luck wherever they might be in September. In closing, he spoke one sentence, "Each and every one, make me proud of you," and Miriam wondered if she was included.

Seven

THE DEMOCRATIC NATIONAL Convention was the most exciting circus in years. Out of the smoke and rhetoric came the nomination of a presidential candidate Cherrygrove had never heard of: an old, familiar name, true, and governor of New York State, but a man about whom little was known. People turned almost plaintively to Heck Hanson as the newspapers began running stories on the man who broke tradition and flew from New York to Chicago to make his acceptance speech before the convention. Another mystery was the photograph of him getting out of the airplane at the Chicago airport, flanked by two sons. What was wrong with him, couldn't he walk by himself? The day after that picture appeared, Heck Hanson sat on the post office bench and told the old men, and a large number of younger ones, all he knew about Franklin D. Roosevelt.

It wasn't much: cousin of the late Theodore Roosevelt, rich, went to Harvard, served as assistant secretary of the navy during the war, ran as the Democratic vice-presidential candidate in the 1920 election, and shortly thereafter was knocked flat by infantile paralysis that left him crippled in both legs so that he had a lot of trouble walking. He could stand up, but it looked as if he had to wear a brace and lean heavily on short crutches. As for his politics and his ideas on how to lick the Depression, anybody's guess was as good as Heck's, but give the man a chance. He had a good look and a fine voice on the radio; with his cocky grin and his air of confidence, it should be worth hearing what he had to offer.

One of the younger men said, "Shit! What's the difference? This country's done for anyway."

Miriam Allen was always grateful that she came to town that morning to buy a new barn lantern. She picked up her father and drove him downtown for the mail, intending to go on to the lumberyard, but she let him out in front of the post office just as Heck finished talking and the younger man expressed his undying faith in the nation. Miriam watched Heck clasp his hands to stop the trembling that had increased during the past year. His hands shook, his heart had begun to miss a beat now and then, but his voice was strong and clear as he spoke directly to the younger man: "Lester, if I didn't know you better, I'd swear you were giving up the ghost. Look at you—no, not just you, *all* of you! Acting like a bunch of old mules coughing in the dust, too far gone to kick the gate down and run over on the hillside where the grass is still green. What are you afraid of? The Depression, drouth, no money? Your memories are shorter than your Dutch courage. We've survived drouth, we've licked hard times, and we never had much money. You know what's the matter with you? You need something to hate, the way old Jake LaMotte did up in Santee County. All the doctors swore he'd be dead at fifty, had heart trouble and asthma and hardly any liver left, but he kept turning up at funerals with the hearse, belittling death in that asthmatic croak of his. Death was the flint that struck the sparks of his steel and kept him alive. He was a better man at seventy-six than most men half his age. He didn't sit around, crying about cruel fate, asking what happened to the cowslips, acting like a charter member of the church of the pointing finger. We're the best, we Americans, at pointing the finger of blame at everything but our own navels, and if we go down this time, let's go down like Jake, let's fall like the old girl I remember who ruled the roost out in the sandhills for nearly fifty years. Queen of cow-and-calf society in Ophelia, she was hated like few women have ever been loved. She rode a big bag of pride that cushioned her like a hot-air balloon, and when they finally brought her down, did she sob and sigh and make excuses? She did not! She swept into oblivion the way a proud queen climbed the scaffold steps to her own beheading!"

In the dead silence that followed Heck's impromptu speech, Edgar Allen spoke to Lester in his mild voice, "And don't let me catch you using dirty language in front of my daughter again."

Miriam drove to the lumberyard, bought a barn lantern, and picked up her father on the way back. She took him home, and then she had to tell Heck what a fine speech he had made. She ran next door and found him in the living room, opening his morning mail. When she finished speaking her piece, Heck said, "That was no political speech, Miriam."

"I know that."

"You can tell the difference?"

"Sure, look at all the practice I've had."

Heck smiled. "When was the first time you heard me?"

"Blackbird County Fair, September 1912."

"What did I say?"

"I don't remember, but you were campaigning for Wilson."

Heck snorted. "Mistaken trust!"

"I thought you admired him, Heck."

"I admired his mind. I didn't like the way he used it after he was elected."

"Well, you can see I've had plenty of practice listening to you."

"Have you got a favorite speech?"

"The day you resigned as county commissioner and announced your retirement from politics."

Heck reflected a moment. "I made no speech that day."

"I know. All you said was, 'I quit,' and then you walked home from town hall with my father and Pat Brown."

Heck looked off through the front windows into the distance above the trees. He did not see green leaves and shingled roofs under a blue sky, he saw life measured through the eyes and mind and heart. Impulsively, he reached out a hand and touched Miriam's cheek.

"Old Bill's a lucky pup. Do you hear from him?"

"Every week."

"Is he getting squared around out there?"

"Slow but sure, he says. Oh, he asked me to find out where the tenth-graders are going to school in September. I know Patrick's going to Bent Fork High School, but the last I heard, the others were still up in the air."

"Vera's grandfather told me she was going to Slayton. Edwin, Ernest, and Marion Dee are all going to Burnside High School. Edwin and Marion Dee will drive every other week, Ernest buys the gas"—Heck chuckled—"at wholesale, from the station."

"I heard about Lionel," Miriam said. "It's too bad he couldn't take you up on your offer."

Heck nodded gravely. When he heard that Lionel was going to quit school and go to work because Mrs. Maas's yearly share from the home farm was no longer enough to support the family, he offered to pay all of Lionel's school expenses, but Lionel refused because even if Heck did put him through the eleventh and twelfth grades, the farm share was still not enough to support the family. Shorty LaFollette offered him a job in the implement shop driving the big truck they were putting into service hauling livestock to market. Lionel was a good driver for his age, and his salary would support the family.

"What do you think, Miriam? Is it the best way for Lionel?"

"Patrick and Ernest think so," Miriam said. "They say he's a natural-born truck driver."

"Let's hope so—have you got time for coffee?"

"I'd better not, Heck. I left Begonia at home, and she gets nervous when I'm gone too long."

"Keep me posted on Bill."

"I will."

"Can he make a quick visit before school starts?"

"He'd better!"

Eight

OFTEN THAT FALL, Miriam caught herself thinking of the last weekend with William Phegley. It had been an affectionate time, with never a display of frayed nerves, and yet it floated into memory with the feel of a sharp rock underfoot. Why was that? Everything had gone so well. They had supper at Heck's, with her father, and William Phegley told them about Ophelia High School and the town proper, how it felt to boss a dozen teachers who made his work so easy it was like taking money under false pretenses. After supper, Miriam took him next door to her father's house and showed him the old picture albums plastered with snapshots of her family, as if verification of the past would magically clarify the future. Finally, William Phegley took her hand and shook his head to signify that he had seen enough Kodak snapshots and heard all he wanted of yesterday's tales. It was time to face their own unsolved problem. He kissed her, the first time anyone but family had touched her in her father's home.

"Have you made up your mind?"

"Not yet."

"The year's started. I've got to get back and finish it, you've got work to do. Keep at it, things will sort themselves out."

"You really think so, Bill?"

"They've got to. We can't let it throw us."

He left it at that, refusing to discuss it again during the weekend. He promised to visit during Christmas vacation, kissed her goodbye at midnight on Sunday, rattled down the lane and turned west on the highway, solid as a rock and intransigent as a ghost, holding her one moment, gone the next. She watched from the porch until the last dust smell died in her nose, and then fall ran on into a winter that seemed endless. Not even the rising excitement of the election eased her tension.

Roosevelt won a landslide victory that forecast a changing future, but farmwork did not change, prices continued to drop, and old people grew older. Charley Lang was failing fast, and Heck stayed home most of the time, sending Mrs. Osborne downtown for the mail on bad days. William Phegley planned on finishing a mound of schoolwork during the first week of Christmas vacation, then driving to Cherrygrove on the day before Christmas, but a storm closed all highways and railroads. By the time the plows pushed the drifts back, New Year's had passed and Miriam faced the long winter haul into spring. She could not visit town on a regular basis, and without the help of the Royce twins, might not have kept her own lane open. She made it into town on the last Saturday in January, took care of all the errands her father needed, said hello to Heck, and had a good visit with Martha. She wished she had not stopped after she saw Charley Lang.

CHARLEY LANG WANTED to live through the inauguration, but as February wore on and it became more difficult to sit through a game of cribbage with Shorty LaFollette, he began counting the hours instead of the days. His last words to Shorty the afternoon before he died were, "Don't disappoint me, Shorty." Charley had always been a blunt, direct man, and those enigmatic words sent Shorty into a state of calm frenzy that lasted through weeks of pondering if Charley meant not to disappoint him by not marrying Martha, or by marrying her. As for Martha, Charley had told her years ago that his will left everything to her because he knew that when she died, she would leave everything to her brothers and sisters or to their children, so that nothing was wasted or disposed of foolishly.

Charley Lang died on March first, three days before the inauguration of Franklin D. Roosevelt. He died quietly, without pain, in his sleep. He was the last of the original pioneers and he was given a funeral that equaled Patrick Brown's. His pallbearers were his sons and Pat Brown, and he was buried a few steps from Patrick and Carrie Brown, beside his wife in the Lang family plot. His children, and their children, forming a semicircle around the grave, constituted a larger audience than the population of Cherrygrove in the early days of the community. While the minister spoke the closing prayer, Pat Brown looked across the grave at the two old-timers: Edgar Allen and Heck Hanson. Who was next?

WHEN SPRING RENEWED the earth, Begonia did not respond with her usual vigor. The change was sadly apparent when Miriam stopped at the lumberyard and watched Begonia touch noses with her son Mickey and followed him out the back door for a tour of the premises. Mother and son were much alike, but Mickey was so full of vim and vigor that Begonia looked half dead by comparison. She trotted rather stiffly beside her son, sniffed his favorite post pile corners, and did not seem to have the heart to join him in natural functions. She returned to the front porch and waited patiently until Miriam opened the car door; it was sadder still to watch her make the climb from porch to front seat in three laborious moves instead of one flying leap. Mickey barked goodbye as Miriam drove away, and Begonia pressed against her in apologetic silence. Miriam knew that Begonia would die soon, just as her father would die and she would go on living; or would part of her die with dog and father, leaving the husk to ponder if life was worthwhile.

Then, thank God, school closed for the summer and as he had promised in every letter, William Phegley arrived to stay the entire three months. He moved into his old rooms at Heck's, and came speeding out to the farm. He hugged and kissed Miriam until her ribs ached, and rekindled old spirit in Begonia, who circled them and barked excitedly at their happiness, feeling so good that she trotted straight out to the hog shed and let the sows know who was boss, with Miriam and William Phegley strolling aimlessly behind, talking so fast that neither understood the other. Finally they embraced again, and partially recovered their aplomb. Begonia escorted them back to the kitchen and curled up, exhausted and triumphant, on her rug. They held hands while the coffee heated and the smell of cinnamon rolls came from the oven; eating and drinking, they grew calm enough for civilized exchange. William Phegley said, "I waved at your father on the way out. How is he?"

"Older," Miriam said, and tears suddenly welled in her eyes. He took her hands.

"Cry if it helps."

"All right."

"Here—" He gave her his handkerchief and wisely changed the subject. "How are the boys?"

"Bigger, nicer. Edwin is helping in the store, Lionel is doing just fine driving the truck. Patrick and Ernest are playing Legion ball with the Burnside team this summer."

"And Marion Dee?"

"Just fine. There's a Legion game tomorrow in Burnside. You've got to come with me, they'll be so glad to see you."

"Wouldn't miss it for the world."

Nine

WHERE WAS JUNE? Where had July gone? Who had stolen August? Driving home from the last Legion game of the summer, William Phegley steered a rough course over the gravel road in his Model A coach, survivor of yet another year, giving off more rattles, adding up more jarring miles through dust and mud and snow and ice, paint peeling, springs crystallizing with age—like himself, growing old but game to the end. He was leaving the next day for Ophelia, to get ready for the new school year, and nothing had been settled.

He did not blame Miriam, and he could not accuse himself. Edgar Allen was losing the endless battle to time, steadily approaching that indefinable point at which resistance slipped unconsciously into acceptance of the inevitable. William Phegley saw it coming but Miriam closed her eyes to the truth. After all, he was her father and she loved him dearly. When he died, when Begonia died, her two strong anchors would slip the bottom of her steady life, and God alone knew where she might drift. William Phegley had arrived in June with every intention of pinning her down, but the first time he saw Begonia and, on several occasions, talked with her father, he did not have the heart to press his argument.

Now they rode through the hot, dusty shank of summer, talking about the game, flushed with the wonder of watching Patrick and Ernest transformed from childhood into the graceful skill and strength of youth. They admired the change in Marion Dee and the way Lionel was supporting his family. They talked of everything but their own unresolved problem on that hot, dusty drive to the farm. William Phegley turned up the lane and stopped beside the yard gate, where Begonia peered through the whitewashed slats and barked her pleasure at their return. They hurried inside, out of the heat, to wash the road dust from their faces and hands. William Phegley took a kitchen chair, rubbed Begonia's ears, watched Miriam put the coffee on; it was now or never.

"We can't dodge it any longer, Miriam."

"I can't decide," Miriam said. "Not until—"

William Phegley finished her thought with loving bluntness: "Until your father dies. I understand, but that's not enough. You have got to make up your mind and set a date."

"Please, Bill. Not now."

"Now," William Phegley said firmly. "I'll put it to you like a semester test. Let's review what you should have learned during the past year. After your father dies, what about this farm? Keep it, sell it, rent it? It's hard to get full value these days, harder still to find a good renter. What about the hogs? Sell them, take them to Ophelia? What about Ophelia? You haven't visited me yet. You don't know if you'll like the town and the people. You have got to find out. When?"

Miriam whisked the cinnamon rolls from the oven and poured the coffee. She took her chair, gave her eyes a wipe, and set her jaw. Her backbone turned as straight as a poker, the strength in her face was reflected in the hardness of her jaw and the glint of her eyes.

"You're right, Bill. I've got to make up my mind, and I will. I'll settle everything by Christmas."

"That's all I want to know," William Phegley said. "Now we've got a date, a time to look forward to. Don't you feel better?"

"No."

"Me neither," William Phegley said. "I won't feel better until we're married."

"I wonder how being married feels."

"Being ignorant of the state," William Phegley said, "we can't go making wild guesses. But it can't feel any worse than the way it is now."

SHORTLY AFTER WILLIAM Phegley returned to Ophelia, Miriam found a full-time housekeeper for her father. Mrs. Larson was a widow who wanted to rent her farm and move into town. She took excellent care of Edgar Allen, met Heck's housekeeper, Mrs. Osborne, and was soon exchanging recipes and playing whist on Tuesday evenings. She imposed a system of regularity that improved Edgar Allen's disposition until he told Heck that the only bad part of having everything done for him was giving him too much time to contemplate a future he no longer possessed. He was doing more reading than he had in years, eating properly balanced meals, and taking more interest in life itself.

How long that condition would last was in the hands of fate. Miriam and William Phegley wrote each other once a week, and within a month after the start of the 1933–34 school year, he was telling her about the Royce twins' uncle Claude Royce, who lived a mile south of Ophelia on the original section of land he had purchased in 1885 when he and their father came into the sandhills to make their fortunes. Uncle Claude had an eagle eye for livestock. He used it to make a good living buying and selling odd lots, feeding stock a week or a month on his own place, always able to find a buyer. Through four decades he had lived in a comfortable house that withstood the blistering summers and fiercely cold winters, sheltering his duke's mixture of cattle, horses, and what-have-you in outbuildings constructed to last a century. He believed in continuity, and it was a shame he had never married, as had his brother, the twins' father, because he was now past seventy and could not live much longer. The twins loved him dearly, excused his faults and underplayed his good points, tried to present him to Miriam, if only in absentia, within an honest frame. In doing so, they gave him an aura of blunt integrity and kindness that was hard to beat.

Miriam was thinking about Uncle Claude's place on Armistice Day, November eleventh. She was working in the big hog shed when she paused to stretch her back and wipe a wisp of hair from her eyes. She looked through the north window and saw a strange dark tinge in the sky; for a moment she thought it was an early storm bearing down but it hung in the sky all afternoon and had come no closer by the time she finished evening chores. It was then, standing on the front porch, that she had the first taste of what it was: dust! Fine dust in the air, come all the way from the Dakotas. But what was it?

She learned in the following days. The papers and the radio were filled with reports of the great black dust storm that swept across Beadle County, South Dakota, carrying so much dust in the air that it drifted all the way to Chicago in one day, and on to New York the next. The past summer had been dry and hot, with subnormal rainfall, but how could so much topsoil get up and blow away in a matter of hours? The truth was, it was the culmination of bad farming practices going back fifty years, season after season of plowing up prairie sod to plant wheat, digging out buffalo grass and putting back nothing one-tenth as capable of holding the earth in place. It was the natural cycle of dry and wet, plow and plant, and harvest, until the land would no longer carry man's mistakes. All was inherent in the newspaper stories and radio reports, and what was clearer to farmers was the shape of the future. The dust storm was not the end, but only the beginning.

Ten

MIRIAM DROVE INTO town one Saturday afternoon in January and found her father in bed. Mrs. Larson drew Miriam into the hall and whispered, "Call the doctor!" So as not to worry her father, Miriam went next door to Heck's and telephoned Doctor Black, who was able to come at once. He examined Edgar Allen carefully, sat with him fifteen minutes, talking quietly about this and that, and only then excused himself to join Miriam in the kitchen. He had that blank expression on his face, the way he looked when he did not want to alarm a family. Miriam said, "Don't soft-soap me."

"Have I ever?"

"No."

"Then brace yourself—," and Doctor Black told her exactly what he diagnosed: Edgar Allen had lived a long, fruitful life and now, with the rare good fortune that came to so few, was simply running down. He was in no particular pain, and clinical tests might dispute the diagnosis, but clinics were not intimately connected with patients, whereas Doctor Black had known Edgar Allen for twenty years.

"He's got that look," Doctor Black concluded. "I've only mistaken it twice. Means more to me than all the tests in the world."

"You mean he wants to—?"

"Never! No, he doesn't know it. I could run him through a

battery of tests, and the results would probably say he was suffering nothing more serious than a little high blood pressure and a hangnail, and when he died during the night, nobody would understand why. Nobody, that is, but you and me."

"Is it his heart?"

"Of course," Doctor Black said, "and his lungs and his arteries and the way his fingers feel and his eyes. Why don't you and Begonia go in and sit with him, that's what he wants. Have you wired your brothers and sisters?"

"No."

"Don't do it now. If I may presume, Edgar told me long ago that when his time came, he wanted you with him, he did not care if the others made it or not."

"All right, I'll wait."

"Good girl. I'll call tonight."

Edgar Allen died the following afternoon at two o'clock. He spent his last hours lying comfortably in bed, holding his youngest daughter's hand, smiling faintly whenever his own thoughts sailed placidly across his face. Once in a while he spoke, and shortly before two o'clock he said, "Bend down," and Miriam put her ear to his mouth so he had no need to strain. He said softly, "You'd better let the others know," and gave her his last warm smile.

Miriam made it through the next three days with the help of her friends. When they returned from the cemetery, her brothers and sisters followed her into the house, took off their overcoats and overshoes, and helped Mrs. Larson make coffee and fill the dining room with all the kindness people call food and brought as a remembrance. They and their spouses sat with Miriam until it was time to leave for home. They faced long drives over winter roads, and they might as well get started because there was nothing more they could do. They had grown up in the community, knew all the people who had become Miriam's friends, and understood that she would feel more comfortable with them nearby than her own flesh and blood. It was not that they had ceased to love her, or that she had stopped loving them; it was just that time had divided them and they all knew it. Their duties, in the shape of their own children, were many miles away. They kissed Miriam goodbye, shook hands with old friends—Pat Brown, Heck Hanson, Jim Lang, Martha Lang, all those who had joined them in the house—and went out to their cars and drove away. They had not mentioned their father's will; if anything proved their affection, that did. Edgar Allen had helped each on his, and her, way; it had always been clearly understood that the home farm was Miriam's. It, the house in town, and whatever else their father left. No matter what they thought, no one had spoken out against what they knew the will would say.

Miriam sat in her father's emptying house until darkness fell. The only sounds were the quiet movements of Mrs. Larson in the kitchen, and the breathing of the old dog beside her chair. She hung on to herself through a light supper, said goodnight, and drove home over the frozen road. She carried Begonia up the walk into the kitchen, slipped on her high-buckled overshoes, and took the lantern out to look at her hogs. The Royce twins had been ever-faithful; the chores were done, nothing pressed her that night. She tramped back to the house, sat at the kitchen table, and had a good cry. She did not cry over her father's death, but for his absence from her life. Mostly she cried for herself, because she had no idea what to do, or how to determine what she should do. William Phegley had been unable to attend the funeral; it was impossible to leave his duties for three days. She understood, and still she missed him. She cried herself out of the tightness in her shoulders, and the knot in her stomach, rubbed Begonia's ears, and went to bed. She knew she would not sleep a wink; she was so exhausted that her eyes closed two minutes after her head hit the pillow.

SNOW BURIED THE fence rows and blocked the highways. Miriam could not get into town regularly; on Easter Sunday she heard a car, stepped out on the back porch, shaded her eyes against the snow-glare of the lemon-colored sunlight, and watched the implement shop pickup plow up her lane into the farmyard. Lionel was driving, Marion Dee sat beside him, and riding the front fenders with Number 9 grain scoops were Patrick and Ernest.

"Crazy!" Miriam called. "You're all crazy."

They hugged and kissed her, and she tried to take them all into one embrace. She led them inside where Patrick knelt beside Begonia and rubbed her gently. Begonia raised her head and licked his hand in recognition, or was it gratitude for appreciating her fight against the inevitable. Patrick sat on the floor beside her while they drank coffee and ate sugar cookies, and told Miriam about school, town, and all the latest gossip. Finally, Patrick said, "How is Mr. Phegley?"

"Fine. He wrote the last time to be sure to give you all his best wishes."

Lionel said, "What about your chores?"

"Don't worry about chores."

But they insisted on helping her catch up on everything unfinished because of the heavy snow. They dug wider paths to the hog sheds, barn, and windmill, made sure the pump was loose and the cutoff working; carried a two-weeks supply of wood and stacked it against the back wall of the coal bin. They complimented Miriam on her hogs, and then it was time to go, sitting three-tight on the cab seat, with Marion Dee perched on Ernest's knees. She watched the pickup lumber out to the highway and turn east toward Cherrygrove. The bright afternoon sun slipped into darkness before the pickup drove from sight.

Eleven

IRIAM COULD FEEL herself live; in the same breath, she could sense her dog's dying. One was a practiced rite, the other could be held at a respectable distance until living became a drudgery. Miriam had told herself time and again that she must not let Begonia suffer needlessly, just because she, the human, wanted the animal to linger on in a kind of cruel reassurance of the human's immortality. As spring came on, Begonia gradually slipped across the threshold of bright living into the drabness beyond. One Saturday morning in early May, after listening to Begonia whimper all night in pain, Miriam faced the truth. She telephoned the Royces and asked if they would do her chores.

"Anything wrong?" Ross Royce asked.

"It's Begonia. I've got to take her to the vet's."

"Can we help?"

"Thanks, Ross. I'll get along."

Miriam wrapped Begonia in her blanket and carried her out to the car. She drove to Cherrygrove and pulled into the gas station minutes after the morning train came through. Ernest and Lionel were standing in front of the pumps, talking with Franklin Krug, who gave Miriam his kind, long-faced smile and said, "Fill 'er up, Miriam?"

"Put in five."

Ernest saw Begonia on the seat and understood without a word of explanation. Miriam's face was all the road map needed. Ernest said, "Burnside?"

"Yes."

"Move over, hold Begonia on your lap."

Ernest opened her door and slid behind the wheel. Lionel got into the backseat and leaned forward to place his hands on Miriam's shoulders. When Franklin Krug replaced the gas cap, Ernest U-turned toward the highway and headed for Burnside. He drove the gravel road at thirty miles an hour, easing around the worst bumps and chuckholes, talking about the weather, how they were getting enough rain for a change, and how it looked as if they might actually have some decent crops this year. Lionel added phrases about livestock and baseball, holding his big hands solidly on her shoulders until they entered Burnside and stopped in front of Doc Jordan's office. Doc turned from the wall cabinet, saw Miriam holding her dog, and came forward to touch Begonia on the head.

"I know it's time," Miriam said, "but I want to be sure."

"Bring her back," Doc said, and led them through the inner door into his examination room. Miriam put Begonia on the table, and Doc talked to her like an old friend—which he was—while his eyes looked and his fingers moved and his ears listened. Finally he looked up at Miriam and nodded.

"It's time, Miriam."

Miriam said, "I'll hold her," and put her arms around Begonia. Ernest and Lionel held her shoulders all through the endless seconds it took Doc to put Begonia to sleep. Miriam did not flinch once. She thanked Doc, carried Begonia out to the car, and they drove the dusty, bumpy miles back to Cherrygrove. Lionel said, "I'll follow you out," and went for the implement shop pickup. Ernest drove on west to the farm, and there were Martha Lang and Patrick Brown waiting on the porch to help Miriam through the day. The Royce twins had finished the chores and gone home to do their own, and Martha had made coffee and washed the dishes, Patrick drying and putting them away. Lionel came up the lane a few minutes later, and they all walked from the house through the grove to the northeast corner where generations of Allen dogs were buried. Miriam said, "Here," and while she and Martha returned to the house to get Begonia, the three boys become young men got the spade and dug the grave.

They buried Begonia among good dogs. The boys waited until Miriam and Martha returned to the house before they filled the grave and patted down the fresh, damp earth. Lionel said, "Should we—?" and shut off his own thought. "What's the matter with me, she'll want to do that," meaning put up a cross or little headstone. They took the spade back to the tool shed, wiped and oiled it, hung it on the proper hook, and walked to the house. They had coffee and rolls and Miriam said, "You've got to get back to town," and when they insisted there was no hurry, she took their arms and made them go. She did not try to thank them; there were times when you did not thank good friends. They felt exactly what you wanted to say, and saved you the acute pain of speaking the words.

Martha stayed until mid-afternoon to make sure that Miriam was all right. After Martha left, Miriam walked up through the grove and stood beside the grave and decided that Begonia should have the same marker the other dogs had: a pair of crossed one-by-fours, with her name and the dates of her life, so that in time the marker would disappear, as other markers had vanished, and Begonia would become a part of the land, unseen and unheard except on the wind in the echoes of her time on earth.

As for herself, prime example of superior, invincible humanity, Miriam returned to the house and sat at the table and cried until it was time to light the lamp. She felt as if the last link between past and future had broken, and nothing in God's world was holding her back from the freedom she did not know how to reach out and take.

She ate a cold supper and prepared for a long night. The Royces came over at seven o'clock to ease her loneliness and bring news that could not have come at a better time: Their uncle Claude agreed with them concerning an idea they had been discussing for more than a year. As she already knew, Claude wanted to sell his place and move into Ophelia, and they wanted more land in western Blackbird County. She and William Phegley wanted to get married. Claude was the key.

"Key?" Miriam said.

"To the trade."

"What trade?"

The twins told her what they had in mind: to have both places appraised. There was no question that her farm was worth more money but they could determine fair value and trade farms with Claude paying her the difference in cash. They would put a good man with a family on her place. She could move to Ophelia and raise hogs on Claude's place, which was only a five-minute drive to town. William Phegley could handle his job as principal of Ophelia High School without a hitch. How did she like the solution to everybody's troubles?

Miriam had never considered such a possibility, but agreed that it was a workable idea. The twins added that Claude had already discussed it with William Phegley, who was eager for Miriam to make her long-overdue visit to Ophelia. She could take a good look at the town and most important, see how she liked Claude's place. His house was not as big as hers, but could be added on to easily, and it had a full basement . . .

"Why, I don't have a basement," Miriam said. "Just the storm cellar."

"Claude's is tight and dry," Ross Royce said. "It's a fine place to keep vegetables and make home brew."

"Which is about all Claude ever used it for," Roy Royce added, with his small, mouth-corner grin. "Inside stairs too."

"Let's see," Miriam said. "When can I get away?"

"Telephone Bill tonight," Ross Royce said, "and saddle up in the morning. We'll take care of things here."

Miriam Allen looked at them. Thinking, she thought, always thinking too much, putting off, delaying, refusing decision. Everything they were doing on this terrible night was being done to make her see, at long last, that now was her last chance. She had done all the thinking a dozen times over, had hesitated and put off and doubted, until life had destroyed all her excuses; and knowing herself too well, if she telephoned William Phegley and drove to Ophelia, and took more time to look at the town and study Uncle Claude's place and meet people, it could end the same way she had ended everything else: in personal disaster caused by indecision.

"No," she said.

"No?"

"I don't need to go," Miriam said. "Call your uncle, tell him it's a deal. I'll call Bill and set the date for the wedding. School's out May twenty-fifth. We'll have the wedding on Sunday, June third."

Twelve

WILLIAM PHEGLEY ARRIVED by train on Sunday, May twenty-seventh, moved into his old rooms at Heck Hanson's, and went to work. He helped Lionel Maas and the Royce twins load the big stock truck with the machinery and tools Miriam was taking along, and saw Lionel off for Ophelia. During the ensuing week Lionel made a second trip to Ophelia with Miriam's furniture and personal belongings, while she moved into Martha Lang's to make final preparations for the wedding. The ladies gave her a shower on Wednesday afternoon; wedding rehearsal took place Wednesday night, with Heck giving the bride away, Shorty LaFollette the best man, Martha the maid of honor, Marion Dee a bridesmaid, and Patrick, Ernest, Lionel, and Edwin the ushers.

The biggest task was resewing Miriam's wedding dress. It had been her mother's and had lain in her cedar chest—now Miriam's—for fifty-four years, with brief outings to cover Miriam's older sisters during their weddings. They were no larger than their mother whereas Miriam was four inches taller and proportionately bigger in all areas. Mrs. Osborne and Mrs. Larson loosened and removed the time-yellowed stitches from the white material that smelled aromatically of cedar and lavender sachet, and gave tangible evidence that dressmakers in the 1870s had not scrimped. There was more than enough material on both sides of every seam and in the hem to achieve a perfect fit. Miriam stood patiently through daily fittings until the job was finished on Thursday morning; in the afternoon she supervised the loading of her hogs and the bay team for their long trip to their new home. Helping Lionel and the Royce twins drive them up the ramp into the big truck, two lines of Edward Lear's "The Owl and the Pussy Cat" kept ringing in William Phegley's head:

> Dear Pig, are you willing to sell for one shilling
> your ring?
> Said the piggy, I will.

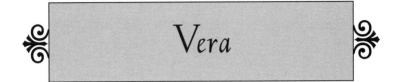

Vera

One

V ERA STENSRUD WAS taller than most girls, big-boned and narrow-waisted, with fine shoulders and breasts. She had a beauty spot, a brown mole, at the right corner of her mouth, and her brown eyes complemented golden-brown hair. Her feet were big, her legs long, and her strong hands were graceful at work or in repose. She wore heavy work shoes, closed-front chambray shirts, blue denim overalls, and pushed her hair under one of her father's old felt hats. In some respects, she was an enigma, even to her parents.

Vera graduated from high school in 1934 and told her parents she'd just as soon stay home and work. A year and five months later she was going on nineteen and still on the farm. Lucille Stensrud regarded her daughter with mock concern.

"No beau yet?"

"No, Ma."

"Can't get rid of you, can we?"

"Not yet."

After the corn was picked that year, her parents left on their regular fall visit to Vera's Aunt Freda and Uncle Bert. Vera rose at her usual time, did the chores, cooked and ate breakfast, washed the dishes, and lazied around the house until it was time to get the mail. She listened to the noon news on the radio and took long afternoon walks; if she cared to, she could drive the truck into town, but there was nothing worth going for. On the last day of pheasant season she took the old Stevens sixteen-gauge on her walk in hopes of getting a nice rooster, but if she missed, which was likely, it would not spoil her day.

Late that afternoon, sun fighting for setting room with a skyful of clouds, Vera was walking the section road on the north side of their farm when she heard birds running ahead of her in the dry corn shucks piled up against the fence. A truck coming toward her stopped, but her eyes were so filled with wind tears that she saw only a watery outline of the driver as he jumped out and signaled her to take first shot. The birds flushed against the wind and flared into a booming turn directly over her head. She fired and missed.

"Vera—duck!"

For a split second, dropping on her hands and knees, Vera knew how it must feel to be shot at, but she was not a pheasant, she could think, and thinking charged her feeling with an emotion strong as the climactic moment of making love, something she had never experienced and was beginning to think never would. The shots came in a continuous roll, the birds cartwheeled across her field of vision and bounced in the corn stubble. Six shots, six birds! It had to be Ernest Stonecifer. She jumped up, mashed the barbwire down with her gun barrel, scissored over the fence, and trotted through the stubble, retrieving. When she returned to the fence, Ernest was waiting, one foot on the wire.

"Hello, Vera."

"Hello, Ernest. Nice shooting."

"Thanks. Headed for home?"

"Might as well."

"Come on."

He took the birds, helped her over the fence, and led the way to his gas truck, breeching his '97 pumpgun before opening the right-hand door, which reminded Vera to break her single-barrel and pry the spent shell case out with her thumbnail before climbing into the cab. Ernest went around the hood, got behind the wheel, and drove the short route to the Stensrud farmyard. Vera started to thank him for the ride, but he was already carrying the birds to the back porch. Following, she called, "Ernest, you don't have to do that."

"We've got plenty."

"You sure?"

"I'm sure." Ernest took off his cap and wiped his forehead. "Where you been keeping yourself?"

"Corn picking."

"How did it run?"

"Right at fifteen."

"That's good. Want some help cleaning those birds?"

"Thanks, Ernest, but I've got nothing else to do."

Ernest smiled and put on his cap. "In that case, I'd better make tracks. Two deliveries left."

He was gone out the lane and north over the hill toward Cherrygrove before Vera could think of anything more to say. She wondered if Marion Dee Potts wasn't coming home much from college, not that it seemed to bother Ernest, he was polite to all the girls and partial to none, and even if he wanted to get married, what would he use for money, being almost the sole support of his family?

ERNEST PARKED THE gas truck behind the station a few minutes after sunset, and went inside to close up. Franklin Krug glanced at the shotgun and frowned.

"How many birds?"

"Six." Ernest sat down at the rolltop desk and began transferring the delivery slip totals to the ledger.

"Well?"

"Well what?"

"Where's the birds? You'll need help cleaning them."

"Gave them away."

"Who to?"

"Vera Stensrud."

Franklin Krug rolled his eyes in disapproval of such antics— not giving pheasants to people who had none, but girls! At times

Franklin was worse than a doting mother protecting her only son from imagined alliances. Tut-tutting, he went outside to drain and lock the gas pumps. Ernest put daybook, ledger, and petty cash into the safe, turned out the fire, and sat on the high stool behind the cooling stove, cleaning his shotgun and smiling at memory of Vera, who did not seem to give a hoot whether she dressed like a boy or a girl. In a dress there was no question about her sex. Other girls made catty remarks belittling Vera; it was pure jealousy of her figure.

"You plan on cleaning that shotgun all night?"

"Go on," Ernest said. "I'll lock up."

"Don't give away any birds tomorrow."

"I can't. Season closed tonight at sunset."

"Heh, heh!" Franklin laughed drily at his own joke. "That's what I mean. Goodnight."

"Goodnight, Franklin."

Ernest finished cleaning his shotgun and leaned it against the wall behind the rolltop desk. He turned out the lights, locked the front door, and stood a moment looking across the street at the darkened hardware store. The wind was up, rain spattered the windows, snow could powder the ground by morning. That meant another slow day, nothing to do but open up, read the morning paper, listen to the noon news, wait for duck and goose season to open. Wait, wait, wait! What were they all waiting for?

Two

VERA'S PARENTS CAME home late that afternoon. They drove the Model A sedan under the machine-shed roof and carried their suitcases and packages across the rain-dampened yard into the house. Lucille kissed her daughter, opened the biggest package, and spilled three rolls of dress material on the kitchen table.

"How do you like that green plaid?"

"Ma, it's just beautiful."

"The minute I saw it, I told Gus it was made for you."

"A dress?"

"No, I thought a two-piece suit."

"We don't have a pattern."

"Oh yes we do—" Lucille opened the flat package and dropped four patterns beside the dress material. "Here we are, all the latest styles."

"Ma, Pa—thanks."

Gus kissed her cheek. "How about some supper before I starve?"

Vera had a meat loaf, sliced beets, and a casserole of scalloped potatoes in the warming oven; after they finished eating and sat back, her father told her what she really wanted to hear.

"Everything went fine, Vera."

"How much?"

"Twenty-two hundred and eight dollars and fifty-two cents."

"Pa, that's good!"

Gus smiled. "Less the kitty, we evened it out at six hundred each. We drew high card for the fifty-two cents."

"Who won?"

Solemn as an owl, Lucille said, "Bert drew a queen."

All the pent-up tension of waiting two weeks ran out of Vera. Gus said, "You two sit, I'll do the chores," and slipped into his mackinaw. He pumped up the barn lantern, put on his wool cap, and went out the back door. Lucille cleared the table and they sat examining the dress material until Gus came back with the milk and a capful of eggs.

"Where'd you get the pheasants, Vera?"

"Ernest Stonecifer. I hung them last night."

"He's a nice boy, Vera," Lucille said.

"And one helluva shot," Gus said. "Now cut that cake."

After angel food and coffee, Gus made his second trip into the night. Vera stood at the big window in the unlighted parlor and watched the lane while Lucille did the dishes, ready on Vera's call to run out and warn Gus. He returned in fifteen minutes, washed his hands, and poured a fresh cup of coffee. Their six hundred dollars was hidden where an army could not find it, just one of many reasons for their continued success in a dangerous line of work. Vera still had trouble thinking of her parents as bank robbers, people like Dillinger, Nelson, and Floyd who shot up banks with tommy-guns and killed innocent bystanders. Vera was proud of the fact that her father had never fired a shot. All it took was what he called horse sense.

Lucille insisted that the seeds of that horse sense were planted when she and her twin sister, Freda, began going with two young men who had graduated from Slayton High School three years ahead of them. They were tall, rangy girls, alike as two peas in a pod, ready to work or embrace sloth. Gus Stensrud was a lanky, tow-headed Swede with a good-natured grin. He was born and raised on a farm east of Slayton and enjoyed the independence that rewarded hard work. His best friend was a chunky, clever-handed boy named Bert Kahler, son of the town's jack-of-all-trades. After graduation, Gus helped his oldest brother who had inherited the home farm, and Bert worked as a mechanic for the Slayton Ford dealer, then moved to Pacific, Iowa, where his parents had grown up, to work in the Packard garage. Bert carried on a long-distance courtship with Freda, grew a mustache, and lost his chunky appearance.

Lucille and Gus were married in June of 1915, and Freda married Bert that August; in 1916, soon after Vera was born, both husbands were called up by the National Guard and stationed on the Mexican border. Early in 1917, Gus was assigned to a new infantry division that wound up in France. Bert Kahler had transferred to the Army Air Corps and went to France with his squadron. Lucille and Freda lived with their parents on the farm north of Slayton, did the work for their ailing father, and watched Vera grow. Their father wanted to sign over the farm to his daughters so he and his wife could retire and move into Cherrygrove, where living was cheaper than in Slayton. Knowing that Bert wanted no part of full-time farming, Freda waived her rights. A few months later Bert's grandmother died and left him a twenty-acre place on the north edge of Pacific, Iowa, one of those in-between properties a family could live on comfortably if the husband had a job. Freda couldn't wait to handle the place while Bert worked in town.

Gus came home in December 1918, helped Lucille and Freda move their parents into a bungalow in Cherrygrove, and settled down on the home farm. Bert got back in March 1919, took Freda to Iowa, and resumed his job at the Packard garage. In the course of time, visiting back and forth, the Stensruds met Bert's Air Corps friends from the Tri-Cities. Les Owen was a lean, laconic man. Nels Nelson was one of those short, bowlegged Danes with melancholy features and a warm heart. They were bachelors and the Kahlers were childless, so all watched Vera grow with great affection.

Vera attended country school, passed her eighth-grade examinations, and began high school in Cherrygrove. Her parents got her a student's license, and she drove the old truck to school in good weather, stayed with her grandparents in bad. During her many visits at the Kahlers, Les Owen taught Vera to double-clutch, heel-and-toe, follow a curve line, gauge width and depth, go into and come out of bad corners. Les had worked on race cars and done some driving, and he offered to bet that Vera could drive and win on the county fair circuit—if only girls were allowed.

When the '29 crash blew the paper millionaires off the high window ledges, and drouth put the capstone on the Depression, crops started drying up, burning up, and blowing away. Bert lost his job when the Pacific Packard dealer went broke. In the Tri-Cities, general layoffs put Les and Nels on the shelf eighty percent of the time. In 1931, the piddling one-thousand-dollar mortgage that Gus and Lucille had taken out in 1926 to buy new machinery came due. The Slayton bank agreed not to foreclose if the Stens-ruds could pay the yearly interest, which they managed to scrape together in 1931, but the only foreseeable solution to their mount-ing problems was the veterans' bonus, hanging in political limbo like a carrot before the starving jackass. They were near the break-ing point in the spring of 1932 when they visited the Kahlers to, as Gus put it, break the monotony of starving to death alone.

Les Owen and Nels Nelson drove over from the Tri-Cities, and they all sat around racking their brains for a way out. Les ab-sently mentioned the bank robbery pulled off the previous day in a town east of Des Moines. The *Register* reported that ten thou-sand was stolen and the gang barely got away because their big sedan was smoking badly when last seen near the Skunk River north of Oskaloosa. Nels mused that if all it took to rob banks was a fast car, they were in the wrong business. Given parts and tools, they could build a car and keep it running smoothly. Lucille said, "That's all well and good, but what about your getaway?"

Nels hooked a thumb at Les. "You forget he can drive with the best of 'em."

"A fast car," Bert said. "And a good driver?"

Gus had not spoken until that moment. "That's just the start."

"What else is there?"

Gus began listing the equipment, the plans, the exploratory travel needed to pull off such a job. The others were caught up in the spirit of the game, and hours later, to their own amazement, realized they had worked out a foolproof plan for robbing banks. It was pure relief when Bert put the silent question into words: "Do you think we could do it?"

Ever the devil's advocate, Freda said, "Could you walk into a bank and stick a gun in somebody's face?"

"Freda, I don't know."

"Could you, Gus?"

"I'm not sure."

"You did it once."

"That was in the war."

"War or peace," Freda said, "the fact remains, you know how to use guns."

Gus looked at her closely. "You know, you just hit the nail on the head. If you know how to use guns, you don't need to shoot. Get me?"

"I get you," Bert said. "I've got no stomach for shooting innocent people."

Les spoke up. "But you've got to scare them."

"And keep 'em scared," Nels added, "so nobody tries to get foxy."

Gus said, "Are you all serious?"

They looked at one another with the wide-eyed innocence portrayed by children on the brink of committing the most outrageous pranks. Gus said, "Let's sleep on it."

ON THE MORNING of the robbery, late in October, the Stensruds and the Kahlers met Les and Nels in Clarinda, Iowa, and followed their prearranged plan. Nels bought a one-way ticket to the bank town and took the noon train south, arriving on schedule at three-thirty in the afternoon. He walked from the depot to the bank, touched his hat politely to the lone teller, and asked if Mr. Johnson had come in yet.

"Which Johnson?"

"All I know is," Nels said, "there's a Mr. Johnson wants to meet me here about a job. You got another bank in town?"

"No."

"Then this is the place. Mind if I wait?"

"Not at all, but we close in ten minutes."

As Nels turned from the teller cage, the front door opened and two men entered, holding large revolvers. The tallest, wearing a wide-brimmed hat and a dime-store false face of papier-mâché, told everybody to keep their arms down and go on doing whatever they were doing. The other man, wearing a floppy-brimmed fedora and similar false face, went through the swinging door into the bullpen, yanked the telephone wires loose, pulled a grain sack from his belt, and motioned Nels to come inside. Nels hesitated and the taller man cracked him on the shoulder with his revolver barrel.

"Get in there!"

Nels got. The other man handed him the sack.

"Fill it up!"

"Huh?"

"Cash drawers first, fill the sack!"

Nels galvanized into action. He emptied the cash drawers, spilling small change all over the floor in nervous haste. He was pushed toward the floor safe located beside the open vault door, and told to fill the sack from safe and vault. The banker and his teller were motioned toward the vault door. Nels started after them.

"Hold on, you're going with us."

Nels quavered, "Please—!"

"Shut up! We'll let you go in a couple of hours. Anybody comes closer before then, we put his lights out. Get me?"

The banker nodded.

"Now get in there—" The banker and teller were pushed into the vault, the door closed but not locked. "Stay put!"

Nels was led from the bank to the Chrysler parked at the curb, engine idling, Les behind the wheel. They got in and sat back while Les drove from town, speeded up, and followed their planned route north on the state highway, west across a river, north on a dirt road that paralleled the river, east over a wooden bridge, and north up a leaf-covered lane into an abandoned farmyard.

Lucille and Freda stood beside the Model A in front of the house. Lucille called, "All clear!" and Les drove the Chrysler across the yard, around the barn, to the edge of the riverbank. They jumped out, stripped off their outer clothing, and put on their old clothes. They rolled up the robbery outfits, revolvers and cartridges in the middle, shoved the roll into a big gunnysack, wedged it into the backseat, and cranked the windows down. They pushed the Chrysler off the high bank into the river; it floated nose-down for a few seconds, then sank in the deep hole. They worked backward from the riverbank, brushing out the tire tracks and footprints. Les drove the Buick from the barn, and while they worked, Freda and Lucille transferred the money from the grain sack to the tire-chain sack and stowed it in the toolbox on the Model A's right running board. Bert finished brushing out his footprints, wrapped the grain sack around an old cultivator blade, and threw it under the back porch. Les and Nels got into their Buick and started the engine. Gus smiled and waved one arm.

"Git!"

Les and Nels drove toward the Tri-Cities; the Model A, carrying two married couples, ambled out to the state highway, turned south, and drove into the town just victimized by bank robbers. They ate supper in the local café, listened to the biggest news story in years, and sympathized with the shorn depositors. After supper, they drove north into Iowa and reached the Kahler place shortly before midnight. They pulled the shades, closed the curtains, made a pot of coffee, and divided the money. It came to one thousand six hundred and twenty dollars, small potatoes compared to larger banks, but they had hurt no one and gotten away scot-free.

———

VERA BECAME SUSPICIOUS when her parents gave her grandparents some money in November and more in May. She cornered her mother one Sunday morning in June. Lucille had a policy of never lying to her daughter about serious matters. She told the truth and concluded, "Do you think we've done wrong?"

Vera said, "Was there any other way?"

"Wait for your father's bonus—"

"Hah!"

"Or win a Bank Night."

"Oh, Ma!"

"That's it! We were at our wit's end. I'm not saying we're right, but I won't say we're all wrong."

"Neither would I. Ma, how did you do it?"

Lucille looked at the gangly sixteen-year-old girl, so like her thirty-eight-year-old mother. Same brown eyes and golden-brown hair, long nose and big mouth; physically close, but closer emotionally. Lucille had controlled her own inner core of wildness, but it was still alive, ready to take a sky-high ride any time she loosened her self-discipline. The same wildness lived in Vera, leavened with Gus's curiosity and good humor. Apparently Vera never gave a thought to the fact that asking how her parents robbed banks was not the moral reaction expected from an honor student who had just completed the eleventh grade at Slayton High School. Lucille exploded in laughter, and Vera joined in, laughing at herself.

Vera's parents took the rest of that June Sunday in 1933 to explain how they went about robbing the right bank in the right town at the right time.

Vera asked, "How did you get enough money to start?"

"Bottom of the sock," Gus said. "Bedrock emergency money."

"How much?"

"Two hundred and sixty dollars grand total."

It was hard to believe they had managed on so little cash, but Gus enumerated certain special advantages. Les and Nels had a small place north of Davenport, with an old barn converted into their own machine shop, and used cars were dirt cheap. They bought a 1928 Chrysler 65 sedan in Illinois, drove it home and rebuilt it. During that time—from the spring of 1932 until the fall—they and the Kahlers looked for, and finally found, a bank that fit all their specifications in a northwest Missouri town ten miles below the state line.

"Didn't Nels take a big chance?" Vera asked. "They saw his face in the bank."

Gus shook his head. "No, they didn't."

"How come?"

Lucille explained that Freda had visited an Omaha store specializing in theatrical makeup and bought one of the kits used by amateur play groups. Freda studied the instruction book and practiced on Bert. By fall she was expert enough to teach Les and Nels how to change their looks without using elaborate disguises. Nels was a heavyset, wide-faced man with a gingery complexion and reddish-brown hair. Freda cut his hair short and dyed it to match a false black mustache; wrinkle lines on his forehead, and the clothes he wore, gave him an entirely different look.

Vera persisted, "Where'd you get all the clothes?"

"Secondhand stores and rummage sales."

"What about the guns?"

"Hock shops," Gus said. "Secondhand stores."

"Did you do the second holdup the same way?"

"No," Gus said. "We made each job look different. That way the cops and G-men couldn't connect two holdups."

In the beginning, Vera feared that everybody in their neighborhood would become suspicious, but she soon realized that people saw what they thought they saw, and all they saw were their longtime neighbors, the Stensruds, working as hard as everyone else, doing what farmers had to do to survive: sign up for government programs, feed whatever livestock they could, keep a cow and pigs and chickens, try to raise corn and small grain and plant a big garden, while fighting drouth, insects, and a falling water table.

They never splurged. They gave Vera's grandparents a minimum of cash, bought groceries in various stores in Slayton and

Bent Fork so that people could not pin down how much cash they spent. If somebody did remark, they had a ready answer: The Kahlers, over in Iowa, best in-laws in the world, were always willing to loan a few dollars if they had the money. But people were so busy keeping their own heads above water they had no time to snoop into the Stensruds' business.

They had survived, in a sense, but in the process they had become calloused by success to the point of forgetting their original reason for robbery: survival.

Three

I N THE YEARS following her marriage, Lucille Stensrud had gotten into the habit of visiting her old high school chum, Inga Anderson, on the first Monday after New Year's, and Inga returned those visits on the Monday after Easter. As time passed, they exchanged little gifts to mark the occasion. The Stensrud farm had a streak of sandy ground that grew fine squash and pumpkins, and the Andersons had a stand of black walnut trees Andy's father had planted in 1880. On the day before her 1936 visit, Lucille came down with a head cold.

"Oh, God!" she fretted. "If I go, I'll give them this cold."

Vera poured her mother another cup of hot tea. "I'll go, Ma."

"You don't mind?"

"Not a bit."

Late the next afternoon, Vera loaded four Hubbard squash and two big pie pumpkins into the Model A and headed north through Cherrygrove to the Anderson farm. She arrived at seven o'clock, helped Andy carry the squash and pumpkins into the cellar, and joined Inga in the kitchen for coffee and cake.

"Ma caught a cold yesterday. She didn't want to give it to you."

"Is she all right?"

"Just blowing her head off."

"What a shame," Inga said. "I was so looking forward to a good visit."

"She said to tell you she'd call next week, and come up later."

Andy came in and poured a cup of coffee. "I put half a bushel of walnuts in the backseat, Vera."

"Thanks, Andy."

"And I'd like to say, 'Let's sit down and have a game of hearts,' but I smell a storm."

"Then I'd better hightail it for home."

Vera left a few minutes later in crystal-clear night; five miles down the road a gust of wind nearly twisted the steering wheel out of her hands. In less than another mile, a blizzard came out of the north and enveloped the Model A, moving with the deadly swiftness that only a high plains storm could generate as it gathered force in the Arctic and moved down across Canada and the Dakotas, blowing fifty to seventy miles an hour, carrying snow parallel to the ground.

Vera stopped the Model A and cranked her window down. She wanted to return to the Andersons and this illogical thought was the beginning of her panic. She opened the door and got out for a look back up the highway, and the full force of the blizzard slammed her against the door as it smashed open to the extreme limit of its hinges. Vera grabbed the doorpost as she lost her balance, the wind nearly blowing her down the road. She dragged herself erect and edged around the open door until she could reach the steering wheel and pull herself into the car. She was plastered with wet snow and shaking uncontrollably with a mixture of cold and fear; it took what felt like an hour to get the door closed and the window cranked up, and then she sat, hands on the wheel, staring into the swirling snow filling the headlight cone in front of the car.

She knew what she had to do, and she was so frightened that she could not move. She was doing exactly what her parents had warned against: losing control and acting like all the other fools who stopped thinking, lost their way, and froze to death. She couldn't help it! Born in the country, veteran of more storms and blizzards than she could remember, and still she was so scared that one corner of her mind was sure she was going to pee in her pants.

And that small thought was the ray of hope. Still trembling, she put her right foot on the accelerator and pressed; the engine responded with a cough, rattle, and bang.

She could not turn back. She released the emergency brake and started down the highway at ten miles an hour, wondering where she was, how far it was to Cherrygrove, how long she could see the road ahead. Wind pushed the Model A so hard that she used more brake than gas, and shifted into second gear to better control the car as side gusts rocked it dangerously; visibility soon shortened to a dim view of the radiator cap and the right-hand shoulder of the road. She was barely moving, wondering how much farther she could go before wandering into the ditch, when she bumped into another car stopped dead in the road. She honked her horn and sat shivering, unable to move, melted snow streaking her face, eyes crying icy tears that welled out and down her cheeks, hoping against hope that somebody was in that car. A lifetime passed before something rapped on her window. She cranked it down and a snow-caked head ducked inside and nearly hit her in the face. Wind ripped most of the voice away. "You all right?"

Vera had to gulp twice before her voice came. "So far."

"Hey, that you Vera?"

"Yes." She finally recognized his voice. "Ernest?"

"That's me—can you follow me into the ditch?"

"I don't know—"

"You got to!" One forearm came through the window and gave her a shake that loosened her frozen muscles. "Stay right behind me!"

Ernest struggled back to his car and drove slowly off the highway into the wide ditch. Vera was afraid the wind would blow her over, but she got her front wheels turned to the right, and half-drove, half-slid off the road into the bottom of the ditch, and felt her bumper thump solidly against the Studebaker's rear bumper. Ernest fought his way back to her window and yelled in her ear: "What you got with you?"

"Chains, shovel."

"Blankets?"

"Two."

"Hand them over."

Vera reached the blankets from the backseat and pushed them through the window. Ernest clamped them under his left arm and slapped her on the shoulder with his right hand.

"Turn off your lights!"

Vera had to think to remember where the switch was.

"Now your engine!"

Vera switched off the engine. Ernest opened the door, took her left arm, and yanked her from behind the wheel. Vera hung on to him while he cranked the window up, closed the door, and pulled her along the side of the cars to the Studebaker's left rear door. He pushed her into the backseat, dropped the blankets in her lap, and slammed the door. He got behind the wheel, turned off his engine and lights, and flipped on the dome light. Brushing snow from his cap and mackinaw, he said, "Where were you?"

"Andersons'—you?"

"Burnside—where did it hit you?"

"About a mile north"—Vera tried to dry her face with her mittens, but the mittens were wet, and all the brushing did was mix melted snow and drying tears into a mess that felt sticky—"I think. Where are we?"

"Got to be close to Jim and Ruth's."

Vera knew there was no use dreaming about making it to Ernest's brother-in-law and sister; the answer was outside, slashing and shrieking, shaking the big Studebaker, forcing them to speak loudly. Vera smoothed the blankets over her lap and dug both fists into the folds to muffle their trembling. She couldn't stop shaking, she must look awful. Why was she so frightened?

"How deep is the ditch, Ernest?"

"About six feet."

"Will it cover us?"

"Should, and the sooner the better."

"Have you got some blankets?"

"Three."

"Is five enough?"

"Ought to be plenty."

"I'm dressed warm."

"Me too."

"How long do you think it'll last?"

"Hard to say. Patrick's grandmother told me the big one in the eighties blew three days and three nights."

"You're kidding!"

"Nosiree."

Vera spoke her thought before she could hold her tongue: "This one better not last that long, I'll have to go to the toilet before then."

Ernest laughed, and Vera tried to join him, but the best she could manage was a grunt. My God! she thought, talk about shot in the pants with luck. If she hadn't run into the Studebaker, she would probably have gone off the road, tipped over, and had no chance at all. She wanted to keep talking, to cover her fear, but willed herself to silence. She bit her tongue, and he seemed to read her mind.

"I'll bet it's over tomorrow."

"I hope so."

"Cold?"

Vera nodded mutely.

"Time to get squared around."

Ernest jacked himself over the front seat and slid down beside her. He unfolded two of his blankets and spread them on the seat, helping Vera rise and turn as he smoothed out the wrinkles. They sat down and covered themselves from head to foot with the three remaining blankets, until only their faces showed. They had on sheepskin-lined mackinaws, fleece-lined mittens, wool caps with earflaps, and four-buckle overshoes. Vera was wearing long underwear and a flannel shirt under her overalls. Ernest had on heavy workpants, a flannel shirt, and a sweater. Finally, Vera had a big muffler that Ernest helped her wrap over her cap.

"Snow's coming in."

Vera could see it in the dim yellow cone light, sifting under the doorsills, around the window frames, through the floorboard clutch, and brake slots. Ernest turned off the dome light.

"Better save the battery."

Plunged into darkness, Vera listened to the wind tear at the car and knew how snow was drifting over the Model A, piling up behind the Studebaker. Storms of blizzard strength blew so hard they often exposed level ground while filling ditches and deep cuts with great drifts of snow; their cars were approximately five feet high, so that once the blizzard filled the ditch with snow, it should grow warmer inside the Studebaker and lessen the danger of freezing.

"What time is it, Ernest?"

Ernest fumbled inside his mackinaw and produced a three-cell flashlight and his dollar watch; the watch read twenty minutes of nine. The clock in Vera's head swore it was midnight. She tried to bolster her own spirits.

"You only forgot one thing, Ernest."

"What's that?"

"Something to eat."

"Did you bring anything?"

"Half a bushel of black walnuts."

Ernest spoke as calmly as a man sitting down to Sunday dinner. "I don't have a pick, but there's a hammer and nails in the toolbox."

"Ernest, you ever pick black walnuts?"

"Not if I can help it."

Vera finally managed a shaky laugh. Ernest added, "If you're hungry, there's a sack of apples in the front seat."

"I take it back, Ernest. You didn't forget anything."

A vicious, curling gust of wind lifted the Studebaker off its springs, threw them into the right-hand corner of the backseat, and with equal abruptness, tumbled them back as the car body dropped; at the same moment, Vera heard a rasping sound.

"What was that?"

"Model A tipped over."

They sat in darkness, listening to the storm build into crescendo, subside, swoop upward again, yelling, groaning, screeching. Ernest turned on his flashlight and brushed a film of snow from their blankets; at midnight the fine mist sifting inside had stopped. He cranked the left front window down two inches. Snow was packed outside, the car was buried.

"Hold the flashlight, Vera."

Ernest crawled into the front seat, unbuckled a trench shovel from the left firewall, and worked it through the window slit. He cranked the window down six inches and angled the shovel blade upward until it broke the top crust. Repeating the procedure through the right front window to create a cross draft, he let fresh air blow through the car for a minute before he closed the windows and crawled back under the blankets.

"Vera, we've got to keep warm and we can't do it all buttoned up. Open your coat."

They unbuttoned their mackinaws and wrapped the flaps together on both sides of their bodies. Ernest put his left arm around her neck, his right around her waist, so that by stretching out across the backseat, they could lie closer together under the blankets.

"Can you wiggle your toes, Vera?"

"Yes."

"Wool socks?"

"Two pair."

"Me too."

"I feel warmer already."

"Good. Try to sleep."

Vera thought that was the silliest request she'd ever heard. She was still frightened, but Ernest's body was warming hers, and in the process making her conscious of how they were lying together and the way she could feel a man's body full-length against hers for the first time. It seemed almost criminal to be thinking such thoughts under the circumstances, but she was, and there wasn't anything she could do about her body's natural response to Ernest's. Then he shifted his shoulders into the awkward corner of seat back and car side, and moved his hips to the left to give his lower legs and feet more room, and Vera found herself lying upon him, her cheek against his chin, her mouth pushed against the corner of his mouth. Ernest said, "You all right?" and Vera said, "Fine," and felt that he was just as aware of her body as she was of his. Her eyes were wide open in the darkness; it seemed a good time to close them and let herself go. Fear had exhausted emotions. Ten minutes later she was sound asleep, dreaming dreams she forgot the moment she woke, ages later, and murmured, "What time?"

"Little past seven."

"Seven!" Vera cracked the top of her head on his chin. "I slept all night!"

"Like a top."

She had not moved from her position above and upon him. He still held her in the cradle of his arms, and their body heat had made a safe cocoon within the blankets. It was as comfortable as lying in bed on a bitter cold morning, only much better, with more promise of life than usually was present when she put her warm feet on the cold rug and braced herself for the act of dressing and dashing downstairs.

"Hungry?"

"Now that you mention it."

There were four apples in the sack. They ate two each—skin, meat, cores, seeds—and thought wistfully of more. Ernest cranked the left rear window down six inches and scooped handfuls of snow into Vera's cupped hands, then into his own. When body heat melted the snow to slush, they had no trouble quenching their thirst. Then Ernest punched a new hole through the crust for air and while it washed through the car he made a rough measurement of the snow depth on the roof.

"About a foot."

"Now what?"

"Wait it out."

Morning was endless, sleep eluded Vera. Sifting snow had dampened the mohair upholstery until it smelled like a wet dog. They sat up in the backseat, blankets pulled around them, and tried to pass the time by playing some of the guessing games learned in childhood, but they were no longer children and, in morning darkness, keenly aware of each other. Vera wondered if the wind would die down by midday; it sounded worse at noon, but just before two o'clock Ernest punched another hole, listened, and said, "It's over, hold the flashlight."

He crawled into the front seat and opened the right front window. Holding the steering wheel, he put his feet through the open window against the wall of snow and began pushing straight out, compressing the snow. Then, using the trench shovel, he worked upward in the snow until he had an opening large enough to accommodate his head and shoulders. He literally dug himself out of the car through the window, broke the crust overhead, and pulled himself into the open. He called, "Close the window, Vera!"

Vera cranked the window up. Ernest dug a trench the width of the door, slid down, opened the door, and pulled Vera from the car. He closed the door, boosted her upward onto the surface of the snow, which had glazed so thickly it held her weight, and climbed up beside her. Vera was disoriented by the pure white landscape until Ernest took her shoulders and faced her east.

"Jim and Ruth's. Let's go."

They were guided by the chimney smoke rising above the grove, plodding along, breaking through the crust, going hip-deep in snow, climbing out, going on; they came from the grove and Ernest's sister and her entire family swept them clean and helped them into the kitchen where it felt unnaturally hot until they took off their coats and caps. Jim said, "How the devil—?" and Ernest started to explain, but Ruth gave him a poke in the ribs and said, "Vera, our pipes didn't freeze, the bathroom's working," and led Vera away.

"Good Lord," Jim said sheepishly. "I never gave that a thought. How about you, Ernest?"

"Outside's fine now, Jim."

Ernest turned to the door and his ten-year-old niece said, "How long were you in the car, Ernest?"

"Since about nine last night."

His niece giggled. Ruth returned, gave her a smack on the bottom and said, "Let Ernest go about his business and help me get a meal on the table, these people are half-starved."

VERA WANTED TO telephone her parents, but the lines were down. Ernest ate quickly and borrowed a scarf from Ruth to cover his face; it was only a mile to town and he could make it easily before dark. Vera was too tired to object; she knew she would slow him down if she insisted on going along. Ernest reassured her.

"If the lines are up south of town, I'll call your folks first thing."

"Don't worry about the cars," Jim said. "I'll flag them."

"Thanks, Jim."

Ernest went down the lane to the windswept highway and headed for town, racing the sun that fell across a clear sky over a white land. He trotted, walked, and trotted, slogged through the drifts, made good time on the open stretches, and came into town an hour before sunset, to be greeted by Franklin Krug who burst from the gas station doorway shouting, "Where the hell you been?" and fussed over him like a mother hen, sweeping him clean, taking off his overshoes and mackinaw, pinching his cheeks and the end of his nose for frost signs, talking loudly, spouting an endless stream of questions that Ernest tried to answer as he rang central.

"Hello, Stella."

"Ernest, are you all right?"

"Fine, can you get Stensruds'?"

"Their line is down, but I can get Keltons'."

Hovering, Franklin Krug said, "What for—?"

"Shhh!" Ernest motioned Franklin silent while Stella rang the Kelton farm and all the party line hooks popped open. Walter answered and Ernest explained briefly what had happened, and asked if Walter could make it over to Stensruds' to tell them Vera was at Jim Lang's place, unhurt.

"If I start now," Walter said, "I can make it tonight."

"Thanks, Walter."

Ernest dropped his receiver on the hook and turned to Franklin Krug.

"Well, first off—"

"First off," Franklin said sternly, "you go on home and tell your mother. She's been worried sick."

AT NOON THE next day, Jim Lang called from the front porch, "Here they come!" and Vera saw the highway department snowplow coming east from town, tossing snow in arcs that glittered in the sunlight. The driver spotted the red cloth on the pole Jim had stuck in the snow above the Studebaker, slowed to a crawl, and carefully plowed the snow off the east side of the highway before resuming his five-mile-an-hour charge. Behind him was the implement shop pickup. Ernest and Lionel Maas got out and signaled directions while Shorty LaFollette maneuvered the wrecker into position above the Model A. Lionel and Ernest shoveled the upper side of the car clear, cranked the windows down, and threaded a two-inch rope around the doorpost. Shorty engaged his winch and slowly pulled the Model A out of the snowdrift onto its four wheels. Lionel and Ernest removed the rope from the windows, cranked them up, and attached the towing cable to the rear axle. Shorty pulled the Model A out of the ditch onto the highway, uncoupled, and drove forward to repeat the towing process with the Studebaker; by that time Jim Lang and Vera had walked across the pasture and reached the scene.

"Did you get my folks?" Vera asked.

"The line was down," Ernest said, "but I got Keltons'. Walter went over right away."

"Thanks, Ernest."

Shorty lit his blowtorch and warmed the Studebaker's oil pan while Lionel checked the radiator, battery, and gas line. Ernest got behind the wheel and hit the starter; the engine coughed furiously, ran on five cylinders, smoothed out, and caught on six. Ernest let it idle while Shorty got down on one knee and examined the Model A's right front wheel.

Vera said, "What's wrong?"

"It hit the ditch bank when the wind blew her over. Let's play safe and tow her in. You ride with Ernest, his heater works."

They put chains on the Studebaker, then rigged the Model A, front wheels up, behind the wrecker. Vera thanked Jim Lang and got into the front seat. Ernest shook hands with Jim and slid behind the wheel. Shorty tootled his horn and led off, and Ernest followed at a safe distance, crunching along in the snow behind the wrecker. When they turned off the highway over the creek bridge and crossed the railroad tracks, Vera was suddenly fascinated by the movement of Ernest's hands—left hand on the wheel, right on the gearshift knob. Watching mere commonplace acts, Vera began to feel them taking on mysterious importance in her mind. Ernest said, "I saw your grandpa and grandma last night, they're expecting you," and slowed while the wrecker pulled the Model A off the street into the implement shop. He shifted into second gear and drove on south two blocks, shifted into low gear, and turned west on the snow-clogged street toward her grandparents' house. Vera watched him gain speed and shift from low into second. She put her left hand on top of his right, felt the vibration of the engine through steel and mittens. She did it before she realized that her left hand had moved, and then she had the stunned feeling that something important had happened.

Ernest stopped in front of the house and moved the gearshift lever into neutral. He turned his right hand over and gave hers a gentle squeeze, helped her out of the car and walked her across the yard, up the snow-covered steps, onto the front porch.

"Get some sleep," he said. "We'll fix the Model A."

He smiled and ran back to the Studebaker, was turned and headed downtown by the time Vera's grandmother opened the front door and drew her inside. Her grandfather came from the kitchen, gave her one look, and said, "What's the matter with you, child, you look like hell struck with a club."

Four

O N THE SAME March afternoon he returned from the annual Bankers Convention in Capitol City, Bob Conklin had a private talk with Pat Brown. The subject was bank robbery and how it applied to Cherrygrove and other small towns. Law enforcement officers attending the convention had awakened the bankers to an ominous new development in bank holdups: Despite the widely advertised fact that the G-men had killed or captured all the notorious bank robbers, more small-town banks than ever were being robbed. Who was robbing these little banks, with such a variety of weapons pushed under the noses of frightened employees and customers? The pros used service automatics, Thompson submachine guns and sawed-off shotguns, but this new breed, called semi-amateur by the law enforcement officers, entered banks waving everything from .22-caliber Colt Woodsmen to .45-caliber revolvers, and there was one authenticated case of a Nervous Nellie sticking up a bank in Maryland with a Signal Corps flare gun that accidentally went off and set the bank on fire.

One night after a poker game at the hotel, the banker from a town in the south central section of the state told Bob Conklin in strictest confidence that his fellow townspeople had decided they would not stand for bank robbery. They planned and practiced a vigorous defense designed to take effect the moment their bank was held up. The heart of their plan was a new silent alarm system that, tripped inside the bank, set off the alarm in the local telephone office and one or more business establishments located directly across the street from the bank. While the telephone operator sounded a general alarm, someone across the street from the bank watched the progress of the robbery and reported on the network of open telephone lines; if the robbers left the bank without a hostage, the final phase of the plan commenced. Expert marksmen waited to pour a barrage of gunfire into the tires, engine, and gas tank of the getaway car. The robbers were given a chance to surrender; if they refused, the outcome was never in doubt.

Bob Conklin admitted that such a plan was drastic, but he wondered if his friends and customers had ever considered the result of a bank robbery in Cherrygrove. He never kept less than five thousand dollars cash on hand, peanuts to big-time robbers, but a great deal of money to the new breed of holdup men. If they robbed the Cherrygrove bank, Bob might not be able to reopen. Was the chance of being robbed urgent enough to tell a few responsible people about this newfangled idea of protecting a hometown bank?

"Let's not go off half-cocked," Pat Brown said. "I'll see Heck tonight and get his opinion."

AFTER SUPPER, PAT Brown walked to the house of his lifelong friend, Hector Hanson. Heck was old and sick, and his housekeeper, Mrs. Osborne, ushered Pat Brown into Heck's bedroom and left him with a warning not to stay too long. Pat Brown moved his chair beside the bed and asked Heck how he felt.

"How do I feel?" Heck waved a liver-spotted hand. "I've been lying here all day, trying to compose an immortal deathbed speech."

Pat Brown smiled. "Famous last words?"

"Earth-shakers, bell-ringers, tear-jerkers. We all try, and we all die the same way, choking, gasping, yelling for help, staring in horror at whatever it is that lies beyond life as it gets nearer and clearer to us. We all dream of famous last words, and all we do is die. What's on your mind tonight, Pat?"

"Bank robbery."

"I'm too old for the action, but I'm a jim-dandy planner."

Pat Brown repeated everything Bob Conklin had learned at the Bankers Convention. In conclusion, he emphasized that he was not asking for criticism of the physical plan. What bothered him was the moral issue. Was it something Cherrygrove could live with, if forced to execute, which in the worst possible sense could turn out to be just that if a carload of holdup men refused to surrender? Money should never be more important than life, but robbing a bank of money that could close the bank and pile more misery on top of the already over-generous dose forced down too many throats by the Depression and drouth—when you looked at bank robbery in that light, it took on an immoral color. Did Heck agree, or what?

Heck pulled himself higher against his pillows. "If a gang robs the bank, and you stop their getaway car, there's only one thing you can do. But don't overlook another possibility. What if they shoot somebody in the bank?"

"If that happens," Pat Brown said grimly, "we stop them any way we can."

"In plain words, shoot to kill right off the bat?"

"Yes, so they can't kill somebody else."

"Just so everybody understands," Heck said, "and while we're on the subject of shooting, this town is too small for indiscriminate use of guns."

"I agree," said Pat Brown. "I want just two."

"Both expert shots?"

"The best we've got, backed up by two good shots."

Heck nodded. "Does away with endangering ourselves. Now, you must give this vigilante action legality. Have the judge and sheriff come over from the county seat and swear-in all concerned as special deputies."

"That's a fine idea, Heck."

"Your cardinal rule must be secrecy," Heck said. "The people directly involved cannot tell anyone—*anyone*—what you are up to."

"We'll see to it, Heck."

"Make them understand how serious it is. Then organize, practice, and pray you never have to trip that newfangled alarm."

PAT BROWN MADE a list of the people he wanted. Through the week he talked with them, two and three at a time, until he was certain they were all in favor of the idea. On Friday night, excepting Stella Olson who had to tend the switchboard, they held a closed-door meeting at Pat Brown's lumberyard. He had asked them to think about ways and means, and it was heartening that all agreed the most important part of the plan was the location of Wilson's implement shop on the east side of Main Street, directly opposite the bank. An awning shaded the big plate glass office window from the afternoon sun, making it difficult to see inside, but creating an ideal observation post from which to look across the street through the bank windows. Bill Wilson, Shorty LaFollette, and Lionel Maas—one, two, or all three—were on the premises during business hours.

The bank had two teller windows, but only one teller. Bob Conklin occasionally opened the second window during rare busy periods, but the cash drawer was seldom used. It made a perfect place to install the silent alarm. Bank robbers always entered a bank's bullpen and yanked open *all* cash drawers; opening the unused cash drawer would trip the silent alarm that blinked a red lightbulb on the telephone switchboard and ring a small bell above the doorway connecting the switchboard room to the rest of the Potts house. The operator on duty—Stella Olson, or one of the Pottses—would simultaneously ring the implement shop, gas station, and lumberyard, so that whoever answered the implement shop telephone could speak directly to the others on the open lines. The lumberyard and the gas station were chosen because everyone had agreed that a gang of bank robbers would investigate every road leading in and out of Cherrygrove and reach the same conclusion: The best getaway route was straight north up Main Street over the railroad tracks and across the creek bridge to the highway. Driving, they would pass between the lumberyard and the gas station, and that brief moment of passage was the time for action.

If the gang took a hostage, the car must be allowed to depart. The safety of the hostage was all-important. But, if they had not forced someone from the bank to stand on the running board, the two riflemen would shoot, and keep on shooting, until they stopped the getaway car, or it escaped.

The number of people involved in the plan was small. They needed no elaborate system; that was why they had voted against installing a red lightbulb and bell in the implement shop. Someone might notice bulb or bell and ask embarrassing questions. Finally, Pat Brown announced that he would pay for the rifles and ammunition. ". . . and that's it in a nutshell. What do you think?"

They thought it was a sound plan. Pat Brown marveled at their calmness while they discussed the pros and cons, agreed that being sworn-in as special deputies was the right way, that a silent alarm system should be installed as soon as possible. Pat Brown interrupted briefly at this point to explain that the alarm company would send two experts in a panel truck advertising adding machine service and repair, who would work after regular bank hours so as not to tip off curious customers. Once the system was installed and tested, they would practice what they hoped to preach by tripping the alarm and driving a car north on Main Street between the rifles aimed by the two best rifle shots in town, Ernest Stonecifer and Pat Brown's son Patrick. They would be backed up, in case one or both were not present, by Pat Brown, Pete Olson, and Franklin Krug, all better-than-average shots.

Five

B Y THE MIDDLE of June there had not been enough rain to
bother a fastidious cat, the small grain had burned up, and
the corn was burning. Farmers estimated they would get
less than fifteen inches of rainfall, and be lucky if the corn ran five
bushels to the acre. Not even the one-and-a-half-billion-dollar
veteran bonus, in checks and bonds, could brighten the summer.
The Democrats were preparing to renominate Roosevelt, the
Republicans were beating their drums for Alf Landon of Kansas,
and a divorced woman from Baltimore was running around with
the King of England. A beautiful new twenty-one-passenger air-
liner called the Douglas DC3 went into regular service, but what
good was that to somebody who couldn't afford a gallon of gas for
his car?

Ernest Stonecifer and Patrick Brown played baseball on Sunday afternoons, and worked every other day of the week. Ernest
and Franklin Krug repaired and repainted the entire gas station,
and Patrick helped Pete Olson in the lumberyard. Summer passed,
school began again, and in all that time Ernest did not see Vera
Stensrud, or forget her.

VERA AND HER father wore out very few pair of two-thumbed husking mittens that fall. Working leisurely, they picked the entire

Stensrud corn crop in four and a half days—less than two hundred bushels off sixty acres. Gus took a last disgusted look at the small pile of yellow ears in one corner of the big crib and told Lucille it was time to visit their in-laws. Vera saw them off on a cool October morning. The next day she drove the old truck into Cherrygrove and stopped at the gas station. Franklin Krug greeted her with his usual long face and kind voice.

"Long time no see, Vera. Fill 'er up?"

"I need gas in the barrel," Vera said. "When can Ernest bring it out?"

"Hunting season starts tomorrow," Franklin hedged diplomatically. "Do you need it right away?"

"Pretty quick."

"I know Ernest's going hunting in the morning. How about the afternoon?"

"Fine," Vera said. "I'll look for him."

She stopped at Showalter's for a box of groceries to give her trip plausibility and then drove straight home. She spent the afternoon washing her hair and dried it sitting beside the stove, reading old magazines. After supper she heated a boilerful of water and took a bath. She had trouble going to sleep, mostly because she could not ignore the perversity of fate. During her two years in Cherrygrove High School, she had thought Marion Dee Potts the nicest of all the girls, and now she was about to do her level best to seduce Ernest Stonecifer. On the other hand, she knew that Marion Dee had not come home since starting college. If she looked at it that way, fair exchange was no robbery.

Morning was punctuated with the sound of gunshots and the unusual sight of dust clouds rising behind carloads of hunters roaming the section roads; at four in the afternoon the gas truck lumbered up the lane and backed beside the barrel on the stand at the front corner of the machine shed. Ernest was unreeling the hose when Vera came from the house.

"Hello, Vera. How many?"

"Hello, Ernest. All the way."

Ernest unscrewed the top plug and inserted the nozzle—
"How've you been, Vera?"

"Fine, and you?"

"Just fine."

"Good luck this morning?"

Ernest grinned. "In Henry Lang's bottom?"

"Oh Lord!" Vera said. "No luck needed there. That must be the best hunting in Blackbird County."

"It is. We filled up in half an hour."

It seemed like utter foolishness for a woman to compete with pheasant hunting, but Vera knew she had never looked better. She smelled a lot sweeter, too, than the last time they were together in the Studebaker. So there she was in a nice dress and shoes, her hair smooth and shining, standing on one foot and then the other, wishing fervently she knew more about luring a man into bed.

"Thirty-one gallons, Vera."

"Come up to the house."

Ernest reeled the hose and followed her across the yard into the kitchen. He wrote out the bill, took the money, and marked her copy paid.

"Thanks, Vera."

"You're welcome. Got time for a cup of coffee?"

"Sure."

"I baked a cake this morning, if you want to take the chance."

"Why not?" Ernest smiled. "Where's your folks?"

"Gone to Iowa, regular visit to the in-laws. There's nothing to do here."

"That's true. How was your corn?"

"Little over three bushels to the acre."

Ernest shook his head in silent commiseration. Vera heated coffee and cut the fresh sponge cake. They sat eating and drinking, conscious of each other in the same way they had been unconsciously aware during the blizzard. Ernest said, "Your hair looks nice," and Vera cut him another piece of cake, wishing he'd say that about her body.

"Patrick back in school?"

"Yes, but I won't hear from him until after Thanksgiving."

"Walter Kelton told me that Lionel's brother and Johnny Showalter started teacher's college."

"That's right, and Julie Wilson too."

"Julie Wilson wants to teach school?"

"She thinks so, right now anyway."

"How's Marion Dee getting along?"

"Fine, I guess."

"Does she ever come home?"

"Too busy." Ernest finished his cake, emptied his cup, and rose. "I'd better get going."

"Ernest," Vera blurted. "What do you think of me?"

"I think you're the best-looking girl I ever saw."

"When did you first think that?"

"Last winter."

"In your car?"

"Yes."

"Why didn't you do something sooner?"

The feeling between them was not a spur-of-the-moment urge. It had been building for a long time, the start buried in time itself that laid down moral ground rules while establishing long-term periods in which to think, remember, and be moved by those memories . . . bits and pieces of chance meeting, innocent words, half-formed thoughts that were worse than half-finished acts, reasons as meaningless as looking at each other with half-felt desire. Everything went into the creation of affection; nothing was too small for love. Ernest put his arms around her and felt her move against him so clearly that he began doing things with his hands that he should not do; by the time they finished their first embrace and flowed effortlessly into another, they had proceeded with red-faced calmness from the kitchen into the dining room and started up the stairs. Vera guided him into her bedroom and knelt down to unlace his greasy work boots and pull them off while he held her head between his hands and wondered absently how she had gotten out of her dress; not that it was important because she helped him out of his clothes and pulled him onto the bed in a rage of fumbling desire.

They made love with the inexhaustible enthusiasm of youth, until windowlight faded and the unheated room chilled their bodies. Lying face to face, smiling, eyes saying wordlessly, We did it, we did it! We didn't know anything when we started, and look how fast we learned! They had nothing to hide, it was easy and pleasant to use their bodies, then admire each other and understand, at long last, the manner in which life's primary function was meant to be enjoyed.

Ernest spoke reluctantly, "I've got to go."

"Can you come back tonight?"

"I'll try."

They were already playing the game according to the local rules. Ernest could call at any time in open courtship, but going to bed opened up a different bill of rights, for which specific amendments must be enforced to keep the neighbors from knowing what was going on. They wanted to stay in bed, but it was late, they were hungry, and routine called. Ernest had to get back to town, with a reasonable excuse for being late. Vera had no lies to tell, but chores must be done, supper cooked, and the evening spent pondering the loss of her virginity. Then, if night passed, which always happened, no matter the sighs of impatience, they had to deal with the next day, and the next, all the days that piled into weeks, months, and years.

ERNEST MANAGED TO visit Vera every afternoon or evening until her parents returned from Iowa on election eve. In that time he discovered that Vera was a good cook, a compulsive clothes picker-upper, and stronger in bed than he was. He guessed that she had learned how finicky he was about personal cleanliness. He had no need to find out what she did every day on the farm, nor did she have to ask what he did in town. They shared a common pool of knowledge that had created the only way of life they knew. The sum total of their exchanged information would have fit handily into a thimble, but even so, they did more talking than was customary for two young people exploring the boundaries of an unknown universe.

Ernest's previous experience with women was rudimentary. If he lumped all the girls he had met at baseball games and dances, a fair composite would have been someone his age who was light as a feather on her feet (or stepped on his feet), wore a pretty dress and too much makeup, and carried on a conversation as substantial as a wisp of floating milkweed. Where was he from, what did he do, did he like the music, the dance floor, her hair, wasn't it hot (or cold, windy, dry, wet)?—a steeplechase conversation in which the hurdles represented everything she wanted to find out about him, while the straightaways gave her time to catch her breath and afforded him the chance to escape.

By comparison, Ernest was thrust into a private world in which he could feel, stroke, and study a body that seemed more beautiful than anything he had ever known; simultaneously, he was happily conscious that Vera was equally engrossed in his body, and such mutual interest invariably led to another expression of affection that never failed to leave them filled with unabated interest in each other. He could run his fingers through her golden-brown hair that spread like a fan on the pillow, and feel the clean white scalp between the roots, while Vera was similarly entranced with his hair, ears, eyes, the shape of his jaw, how his teeth fit together, and the way she could put her toes on top of his toes and be lifted into and against him. They could hold their palms together, look into each other's eyes at a range of two inches and experiment until they achieved the most comfortable position for their noses, so that an embrace could be maintained indefinitely.

They began to anticipate simple thoughts, movements, even words. They could lie together and rediscover all the recently traveled curves and hollows of their bodies, go downstairs to eat and drink, where the smell of coffee and kitchen seemed sharper and more attenuated. Discovering this strength of interest made them comprehend vaguely that their minds, filled with a kind of inverse shyness, were harder to open and give freely of. And all the time, in every way, they sensed that their shared magic had been repeated an infinite number of times by an infinite number of people; had been, was, and would always be, without end, an act that transported, entranced, and briefly blotted out the hard, never-ending business of existence.

Six

THE ELECTION KEPT Pat Brown so occupied that he did not remark on the change he had noticed that fall in Ernest Stonecifer, even to Pete Olson, who had probably spotted it sooner. But now that the election was over, it was restful to contemplate local problems. Pete mentioned Ernest just before closing time on Wednesday afternoon; in his best oblique fashion, Pete zeroed in on Ernest by way of the past.

"Pat, do you think Ernest's gotten over Marion Dee?"

Pat Brown looked up from the ledger. "Yes, don't you?"

"Looks like it."

"Then what's the argument?"

"Looks like Cupid's hit him in the pants again."

"Who?"

"I don't know."

"Better ask Franklin."

Pete smiled and trotted across the street to the gas station, where Franklin was closing up.

"Where's Ernest?"

"Said he was going east."

"This late?"

"He's trying to find good stubble for geese."

Pete warmed his hands over the stove and spoke blandly, "I wonder who she is?"

Franklin could make his face as smooth and expressionless as the oval surface of an egg. He met Pete's questions with guileless blue-eyed innocence, and betrayed Ernest in the very fact of trying to protect him.

"I knew it," Pete said. "He's got a new girl!"

Franklin smiled. He had guessed a week ago and held his own counsel while he watched, weighed, and tried to ascertain the girl's identity. Franklin respected Ernest's right to privacy but he could not resist the challenge. Checking daily mileage on the gas truck against exactly known distances to all delivery points, Franklin soon determined that Ernest was making legitimate deliveries to farms north, west, and east of Cherrygrove. Discrepancies appeared on the trip tickets to farms south of town. Franklin had carefully reviewed his mental list of likely candidates living south of town, and concluded that only one filled the bill.

"Yes," he said. "I think so too."

"Who is she?"

"I'm only guessing."

"Has he been seeing her often?"

"Ever since hunting season started."

"Which way from town?"

"South."

Pete Olson clapped his hands. "I knew it! Vera Stensrud!"

"Can't be anybody else."

They did not pursue the most delicate question: How far had the supposed affair progressed? It was not polite to assume that the young people were sleeping together. That was insulting them without proof.

Seven

ERNEST CALLED ON Vera Saturday night and met her parents. He was not meeting total strangers, but the extent of their acquaintance in the past had been limited to saying hello in town or at baseball games. Now he shook hands and sat in the dining room, drinking coffee and eating angel food cake, telling them that three bushels of corn to the acre was the local average, and Henry Lang said just the other day that 1936 was sure as hell going down as one of the worst years on record. Gus asked about next year's baseball team—was it true that Lefty Jackson had been offered a better deal by a town in the southeast corner of the state?

"Sure," Ernest said. "They offered Lefty a year-round job in town at eighty dollars a month, free room and board, plus ten dollars a game, win or lose, and the privilege of accepting pitching offers during weekdays if he doesn't strain his arm."

Gus whistled. "Will he take it?"

"He's thinking it over."

"What's there to think?" Lucille said. "He can't lose."

"That's what Pat says," Ernest said. "He told Lefty to think about the time when he can't pitch anymore."

Lucille said, "Is he married?"

"No, and not going to be. Who can?"

"That's true," Gus said, and grinned. "Well, here we are, talking your leg off, like all parents. Is there a dance someplace tonight?"

"No," Ernest said, "but I thought we'd see a movie."

"I'll get my coat," Vera said, and went into the front hallway. Ernest shook hands with Gus and Lucille and when he opened the front door for Vera, Lucille said, "I hope it's a good movie," and Gus called after them, "We'll probably be in bed when you get back, Ernest, so we just want you to know, you're welcome any time."

"Thank you," Ernest said. "Goodnight."

Walking to the Studebaker, Vera squeezed his arm so hard it hurt, and before Ernest could start the engine she was kissing him and talking between her teeth, "I almost died waiting!" She kept on touching him and kissing him, all the way down the lane, and south to the Slayton–Bent Fork highway before she sat back.

"My folks are happy at last."

"Why?"

"Because I'm finally showing some interest in a man—and you see how they feel about you."

"I'm glad about that, Vera."

"So am I," Vera said, "but it won't make things any easier for us."

Ernest knew what she meant. They had talked it over at length one night, lying in bed, and agreed that making love in the backseat of a car was not the way they wanted to keep company.

EVERY PASSING WEEK brought them nearer the bad winter weather, during which they would be lucky to see each other twice a month. A week before Christmas they went to a movie in Bent Fork and returned via the main highway to Slayton and north through the hills. Sitting close, Vera began revealing her secret hopes and dreams. "I used to study the geography maps. Did you ever wonder what it was like in China, Africa, India?"

"Once in a while."

"All those faraway places where the climate's different and

people are black, brown, and yellow. When I got older and started the ninth grade in Cherrygrove, I spent a lot of time reading the *Blackbird County News*, but I loved reading the *Omaha World Herald* when my folks bought one in Slayton after church. All those funnies and that section full of pictures of people and places. My God!"—Vera sighed—"the longest trip I've ever taken is visiting my aunt and uncle in Iowa. You know what I dream, Ernest?"

"What?"

"That some day I'll turn my face and follow the setting sun all the way to the Pacific Ocean. Do you ever dream of going somewhere else, Ernest?"

"Once in a while."

"Where?"

"Just places."

"Ernest, let's go to California."

Ernest laughed. "Everybody wants to go to California."

"All right, let's go to Oregon, Washington. I don't care, I just want to go see what it's like and do something else for a change. Don't you?"

"At times."

Vera ran her left hand up his neck and cupped it over his head. "My folks told me once if I ever wanted to do something real bad, to go ahead and shoot the works. They said there ought to be one time in everybody's life when you say the hell with the cost, go ahead and do it, because you might not get a second chance."

Ernest stopped the car on the crest of the next hill and looked at her. "You're serious."

"You're damned right I am!" Vera said. "I've got forty-four dollars saved up. That's not enough to go to California, I know that, but let's spend it all next summer on something we want to do. What do you say, Ernest? Let's do it!"

Eight

WINTER CONSPIRED HATEFULLY against Ernest and Vera, covering the country roads with snow, then kicking up high winds that blew the plowed snow back into the cuts. They saw each other three times between New Year's and the first Saturday night in March. Those weeks of denial gave Ernest time to test his willpower and decide that he could do without Vera only because he would see her in the spring. Vera was made of equally strong stuff, but she inclined to explode at the end of their involuntary separation. She swarmed all over him that Saturday night before he drove from the farmyard, and only their mutual dislike for backseats kept them from murdering continence. Three weeks later, on Saturday night, March twenty-seventh, Vera told him that her parents were leaving for Iowa the next morning on a three-week visit.

"Think of it," Vera said. "Three whole weeks!"

Ernest could understand why the Stensruds were eager to take a trip, but had they guessed how far he had gone with their daughter? If they suspected, they gave no sign. They were as nice as parents could possibly be to a young man who dared not entertain serious intentions because he could not afford to get married. Even under those trying circumstances, they made him welcome. Ernest brought Vera home early that Saturday night, shook hands with her parents, and wished them a good trip.

VERA ROSE EARLY on Sunday morning, cooked breakfast, and saw her parents off for Iowa. The last thing Lucille said as she got into the Model A was, "Have a good time, dear, and be careful!"

That night, lying together in Vera's bed for the first time in nearly five months, Vera said, "Ma knows."

"Knows what?" Ernest mumbled sleepily.

Vera gave him a shake and jumped out of bed. Ernest followed her downstairs, buttoning up his shirt and pants, calling, "What do you mean, she knows?"

"She's my mother." Vera put the coffee on.

"How about your father?"

"He's bound to. They don't have any secrets."

Ernest sat at the kitchen table and worked his toes into the small rag rug under his bare feet. If her parents knew, how could they go away for three weeks and leave the two lovebirds alone? Was it a trap? Would they come sailing into the yard, burst into the house, and shout, "Aha! We thought so, what are you going to do about it?" The picture was so vivid in his mind that he had to laugh. Vera turned from the stove.

"What's the joke?"

Ernest told her. Vera sat on his lap and laughed louder than he did; then she poured the coffee and told him that her parents would never do a thing like that, they trusted her.

"Now *that's* really funny!"

"But it's true."

"Then how do they feel about me?"

"They know I'm crazy about you," Vera said, "and they know you've got to help take care of your mother and kid sisters for a while. But that's all right, they know I don't want to get married."

Ernest stopped eating in mid-bite. "You don't?"

"Neither do you."

"I never said that."

"I know you didn't, but you don't hear me kicking, do you?"

"It's different from saying you don't want to *get* married."

"No, it's not," Vera said. "I'm just being honest. Does that scare you?"

"No."

"Then finish your cake. I'm getting cold."

Later, lying with her tousled head on his chest, her breath warming his chin, Ernest remembered her words. Saying she did not want to get married was, in an odd way, a fleeting insight into her character. It was only a glimpse, but it was the first of many sure to come as they grew more intimate, not physically but with the unconscious closeness of young lovers who gradually learned so much about each other that the time came when they knew too much to go on.

GUS AND LUCILLE returned from Iowa on Sunday, April twenty-eighth. One look at their faces told Vera everything had gone wrong. She did not have to wait for the bad news; telling her what had happened seemed to ease their pent-up anger. The bank (they explained) had all the earmarks of a pushover, but looks were deceptive in the spring of 1937. They waltzed inside, stuck up the three employees and lone customer, and headed for the money only to discover that the vault door was closed and one of the new time locks was set for nine o'clock in the morning. They scooped the cash from two teller windows and the round floor safe; at that moment Les sounded his horn, the signal to drop everything and run.

"What happened?" Vera asked.

Lucille said, "Somebody up the street gave the alarm."

Gus would not admit it in so many words, but Vera had the feeling that escape had been touch-and-go until rain fell in sheets, darkness closed in, and they made their getaway.

"How much did you get?"

"Five hundred and three dollars," Gus said. "Figuring our costs, we netted thirty-six. That's worse than farming."

Vera wished she could read a local newspaper account of the holdup. She had the feeling that, for the first time, her parents had not told her everything. Lucille regained her composure in a week, but Gus remained stony-eyed throughout the dull routine of spring work until he sweated out his anger and found a wry smile.

TWO MILES WEST of Stensruds', on a stretch of north-south section road no one drove at night, the highest hill in the area afforded a grand view of stars and sky. A week after Gus regained his sense of humor, the Studebaker was parked on top of the hill, driver and passenger sitting on the front fenders, holding hands across the radiator to emphasize that bodies might demand more license but common sense ruled the night.

"Listen," Ernest said, "would your folks mind if I took you along this summer on some of our hired games?"

"No, but what about Patrick?"

"What about him?"

"Playing baseball for money is strictly business," Vera said. "You told me that yourself. Maybe Patrick wouldn't like me tagging along."

"He won't mind." Ernest smiled. "Tell you the truth, I think he'd like to have you. There were times last summer, we were so damned tired we hated to drive home."

"I knew it! All you want is a driver."

"Why, sure!"

Vera slid off her fender and came around the hood, pushed between Ernest's legs, and put her arms around him. They held each other, familiar as blood and bone, silent as the night.

Nine

G US AND LUCILLE had not told Vera the entire story of the aborted April holdup. Gus had pistol-whipped one of the tellers and taken the bank president hostage on their running board in order to get out of town. They dumped him two miles north and forgot all about him in the getaway, but next day's *Des Moines Register* related how he was picked up by a passing car, wet and cold in the rain, and suffered a heart attack later that night in the hospital. Kidnapping was added to the other charges already filed against the four unknown John Does who escaped. Should the banker die, it would become second-degree murder.

That was more than enough to make sensible people call a halt, but they had lost sensibility, let alone reason. Through the spring and early summer, Gus and Lucille worked hard, went nowhere but Slayton to shop, and slowly lost their biased feeling of being cheated. They looked forward to harvesting a modest crop of oats, and nursed hope for the corn, but rain slacked off late in June and fell with that maddening persistence that forecast a yield somewhere between poor and fair, meaning about ten to fifteen bushels per acre, just enough to keep hope alive but not enough to feed a family.

They knew it must stop, and they could not stop searching for another bank. A safe bank, a fat one, a cinch! Les and Nels looked, Bert and Freda looked; by the middle of June their short homey letters expressed the results: There was not a *safe* bank left in their territory. They had overworked their welcome. They cast about for alternatives, knowing full well that habit had already made the decision: They *had* to rob another bank.

ON THE FOURTH of July weekend, Ernest and Patrick drove eighty miles southwest to play for Hollister in the first game of a three-day celebration, and invited Vera to come with them. Ernest went four for four, handled eight chances and stole third base in the last of the ninth inning with the score tied and two away. His base running upset the pitcher so badly that he walked the next batter and was forced to pitch to Patrick, who promptly hit an inside fast ball over the left field fence for three runs and the game.

They showered and changed clothes in a dressing room set up for hired ballplayers in the basement of the bank, and as they came up the outside steps, smiling fans stuffed paper money into their shirt pockets. Eating supper in the restaurant across the street, they smoothed out the bills and added the totals and Vera learned how generous baseball fans could be after winning large bets on their team. Ernest had sixty dollars, Patrick counted fifty-five. They had been paid fifteen dollars apiece, plus ten dollars' traveling expenses, to play the game. Vera's eyes shone.

"That's seventy-five for Ernest, and seventy for you, Patrick!"

Patrick grinned. "Supper's on me."

Ernest said, "Not by a damn sight," but their argument was academic when the restaurant owner refused their money and made them accept a pound of his finest homemade peanut clusters to tide them over the long drive home. Patrick slept all the way to Stensruds' farm, woke to say goodnight to Vera, and moved into the front seat. Driving the last familiar miles, Ernest said, "We could get wrong ideas about a day like this."

"The money?"

"How many games have we played for money, last year and so far this?"

"I never added them up."

"Fourteen last summer, five so far this year. How many times did we get a bonus?"

"Twice," Patrick said. "Ten dollars from Upland last year, and today."

"Twice," Ernest said. "Now just remember, I couldn't take time off to play these games if Franklin wasn't so decent about doing all the work. What I mean is, I like playing and making some extra money, but I wouldn't want to try doing it for a living, would you?"

"No."

Ernest came to the point he had so judiciously approached. "Then what are you going to do?"

"Do?"

"Your trunk. I saw you and Pete haul it up to your house from the depot. You've got one year of school left, but you're not going back, are you?"

"No."

"Want to talk about it?"

"Not yet."

" 'Nuff said."

ERNEST WAS PUZZLED by Vera's obsession with Amelia Earhart's disappearance over the Pacific on the same night they had driven home from the game at Hollister. She talked about it for days, rattling off the log of Amelia Earhart's famous flights. She had never talked to anyone about Amelia Earhart before, the lost lady who was the symbol of her own unfound freedom, the shining example of what a woman could do when she had the courage to try. Vera knew where Amelia Earhart was born, how she learned to fly, and when she married the millionaire who gave her the chance to spread her wings. Vera talked about Amelia Earhart on the night of July fourth, sitting with Ernest on their hilltop two miles west of the farm.

"May twentieth and twenty-first," Vera said. "You know what those dates represent?"

"No."

"Her solo flight across the Atlantic in 1932. Remember Lindbergh's flight in 1927?"

"Sure, everybody does."

"He crossed on the same dates. I'll bet she did it on purpose."

"Why?"

"To show the world she could fly as good as a man."

Then Ernest remembered Vera in Cherrygrove High School, bent over her desk, eyes narrowed in concentration, right hand gripping her pencil so tightly the knuckles showed white. That was the way she studied, the way she poured her fierce energy into everything she cared about, including love. Now Ernest understood why she kept the childhood airplanes in her room, all sizes from one-inch pot-metal peewees to real flyers with rubberband motors. He could picture Vera working at her table by the light of a Coleman, the smell of banana oil filling the bedroom as she cut, fitted, and glued, staring beyond the balsa wood, cloth, and glue into her own private dreamworld of real airplanes.

Unexpectedly, Vera said, "Patrick's not going back to school."

"It's true," Ernest admitted, "but don't bother him about it."

"God no!" Vera said. "I can guess what he's trying to figure out. What to do, where to go, stay here, go there, but where? I'm in the same boat!"

"Still dreaming about California?"

"Never stopped," Vera said. "Why don't you try it?"

"Can't afford it."

"You've got to," Vera said fiercely. "If you don't believe you can do something, what's the use of trying anything? You wait and see. I'll surprise you one of these days."

"With what?"

"A good idea."

Ten

AUGUST RAN ITS hot, dry course of exaggerated importance, pushing up momentous molehills from the dust.
Patrick told Ernest and Lionel Maas that he had decided
to go to Seattle in the fall, and they had a long talk about the State
of Washington. Ernest told Vera the news that Saturday night.

"When will Patrick go?"

"Right after hunting season."

"To work and play baseball next summer?"

"That's his idea."

"Why don't you go too?"

"Can't be done."

"Why not?"

Ernest owed so much to Jim Lang that any thought of leaving
seemed worse than turning traitor to his country. Not that Jim
would stand in his way if he wanted to go. His departure would not
hurt the gas station business and Franklin Krug could run things
just as efficiently as he supposedly had, until they could find a new
manager. But he could not go, and he tried to explain himself in
terms that Vera understood clearly.

"It's the money."

"If I could get the money," Vera said, "would you go?"

"That's a pipe dream."

"Let me smoke it," Vera said. "How much would we need?"

"You tell me."

"To make the trip, find work and a place to live? I'd say five hundred."

Ernest stared at her in the moonlight. Where in God's name could she get five hundred dollars? He had played extra baseball games all summer to earn, at most, two hundred. What could Vera do? It was wiser, and kinder, to humor her.

"All right, I'll think about it."

Vera threw her arms around him and began kissing him in an almost frantic outburst of affection that continued until she kissed him goodnight and ran into the house. She poured herself a cup of coffee and joined her parents at the kitchen table. Lucille offered a half-hearted smile.

"Ernest have a game this week?"

"Labor Day. Ma, I've got an idea."

"Shoot."

Gus looked up from *Capper's Farmer*. "Shoot me first, put me out of my misery."

"Ma, you know I want to go to California."

"We know it," Lucille said, "but we can't swing it right now, dear."

"Ernest said he'd think about going if we could raise the money."

Lucille smiled. "How much?"

"Five hundred."

Gus dropped his magazine. "Jesus!"

"Would you let me go if we had five hundred?"

"Let you?" Gus said. "If we had a thousand, we'd pack up and go along."

"What about the farm?"

"It's free and clear now," Gus said. "All we've got to do is pay taxes and insurance. We'd rent out the land on fair shares, hang on to it until things got better, and then sell."

Vera said, "I know where you can get a thousand."

"Where?"

"The Cherrygrove bank."

Vera waited for the explosion, but it did not come. Gus looked at her and folded his hands, Lucille started to say something, changed her mind, and took a long sip of coffee. Gus finally said, "You know the rule about hometown banks."

"I know, Pa, but name a better one."

"The others would throw a fit."

"No they won't," Vera said. "Not when you tell them about the bank, and show them how to do it."

"Just like that?" Gus said. "Fine, you show us, so we can show them. Go on, the floor's yours, show us how easy it'll be."

"First off," Vera said, "Mr. Conklin always keeps at least five thousand dollars in cash on hand."

"How do you know?"

"People talk, I listen. I know Mr. Conklin keeps that much. There's just him and Emma in the bank. They always open the vault and that old round safe every morning and never close them until just before they lock up for the night. And if you just think about it, you'll see how easy it is to get away slick and clean."

"Whoa!" Gus said. "Rob the bank first."

"That's your business," Vera said. "I don't see anything so hard about driving up front, robbing the bank, and getting out of town. Come in from the south, go out north over the railroad tracks to the highway, and turn west—"

"West?"

"Sure, because everybody'll expect bank robbers to turn east to-ward Sioux City, or head north for Highway 20. I'd fool 'em, turn west, and double back to the farm."

"You've got a full head of steam," Gus said. "Don't waste it."

Vera grinned. "I'd go three miles west on the highway and turn south on the Summer Lake road four miles and turn east. Meet Ma and Freda two miles west of the farm. Pa and Bert get into the Model A with them, take all the stuff along, and go straight back to the farm. Nels and Les drive south a mile, east a mile, and back north on the section road. I'll loosen the fence the day before; all they have to do is let it down, drive over the wire into our west pasture, and come straight through the fields to the gully behind the barn. Hide the car in the barn or the machine shed. They can leave that night. Bert and Freda can stay as long as they want—they're not hiding anything."

"Sounds easy," Gus said, "but what about Bob Conklin and Emma? They know me."

"With a mask on?" Vera said. "I don't see how."

She rinsed out her cup and went upstairs to bed. Next morning Lucille served her pancakes and sausage for breakfast.

"What's the special occasion, Ma?"

"Your plan," Lucille said. "We've been racking our brains all summer, trying to find a bank, and you put your finger on it right under our noses. Gus couldn't sleep last night. He went out for a walk at four A.M., came back at five, woke me up, and said let's do it. We're going over to Bert and Freda's right after Labor Day and tell them."

"Where's Pa?"

"Drove over to Slayton to mail the letter we wrote Bert and Freda at six A.M. Eat your breakfast, we've got work to do."

THE LAST WEEK of September was blissful for Vera and Ernest. Her parents drove to Iowa, and during those seven days Vera never let Ernest forget that she was getting ready for the trip to California. She told Ernest that her parents would try to borrow the money from her aunt and uncle. Ernest could not understand how they had saved five hundred dollars, but Vera explained in glowing general terms that Bert was a smart man who kept a lot of irons in the fire. She reminded Ernest that her personal savings had grown to fifty-six dollars, and she knew he had saved money during the summer.

"How much from baseball, Ernest?"

"A little over two hundred."

"How much a month do your folks need?"

"It varies," Ernest said. "More during the winter for heat."

"Your pa's on WPA now. That helps a lot."

Ernest nodded. His father was acting timekeeper for the local crew made up of men from Cherrygrove and the southwest corner of Blackbird County. He spent most of his time in the truck cab that transported the crew from town to the various projects repairing bridges, culverts, road signs, and other odd jobs in the west end of the county. His pay took care of the monthly grocery bill but all other expenses were Ernest's responsibility. Vera knew that, but she added, "You can send money from California. I'll help you."

When she persisted too vigorously and Ernest lapsed into good-natured silence, it was time to make love. Vera knew him so well that she could play upon his emotions, but just when she thought she was controlling his reason, he did not respond. He was as affectionate as ever, gently caressing her body, making love with undiminished enthusiasm, but he never actually promised that he would cross-his-heart-and-hope-to-die go to California. When her parents returned from Iowa, Vera wondered if abstinence would influence Ernest's final decision. Everything depended on how persuasive Gus and Lucille had been.

They came home October second, and their faces told Vera all she wanted to know before they kissed her and started talking. They had convinced everyone in Iowa, they told her, that the idea was better than any job pulled in the past, simply because it was so unexpected from the standpoint of the Cherrygrove bank and because they were so intimately connected—and acquainted—with, bank, town, and every mile of road. When Gus laid out the plan, their vote was unanimous. Not only that, there would be no delay while Les and Nels bought and prepared the getaway car. They had spent the idle, late summer and early fall doing just that on the hunch that Gus or Bert would come up with a feasible plan. There was nothing left to do but pick the date.

Vera said eagerly, "Did you do it, Pa?"

"Monday, October eighteenth."

Vera knew that hunting season opened on Saturday, the sixteenth, and Gus went on to explain that Bert and Freda would time the drive to arrive at three in the morning on the sixteenth.

Les and Nels would leave their Buick in Iowa and follow Bert and Freda all the way in the getaway car; north of Slayton Freda would change seats with Nels, and while Bert and Nels drove on to the farm, she would guide Les along the section roads to the west side of the farm, let down the loosened fence, and bring the getaway car across the pasture into the gully behind the barn where everyone would pitch in to hide it.

"Where, Pa?"

"What do you say to putting it behind the threshing machine in the machine shed?"

"Good idea," Vera said, "and use the big tarp?"

"That's the ticket," Gus said. "Now, we'll do some hunting Saturday afternoon. Les and Nels will stay undercover, with you in the house, Vera. We'll drive the getaway route until Bert and Freda know it by heart. Nobody'll pay any attention to us on the opening day of hunting season with all those cars on the roads. Vera, it's up to you to make sure Ernest don't hang around that Saturday night, and it would help a lot if you don't see him on Sunday. Can you drum up a good excuse?"

"Don't worry, Pa. I'll take care of it."

"Fine, then all we have to do is go into town Monday afternoon about four o'clock and withdraw five thousand dollars from Bob Conklin's bank."

Eleven

O N SATURDAY NIGHT, Ernest met Vera's Uncle Bert and Aunt Freda, swapped some hunting news with Gus, and said goodnight when Vera came downstairs. She smelled of dry cornhusks and dust, and he felt tiny flecks of husk in her hair when it brushed his cheek. Her hands, even protected by husking mittens, had begun to roughen.

"I'm sorry," Vera said. "I didn't have time to take a bath."

"You're not dirty."

"The damned corn is choked with summer dust."

"How's it running?"

"Almost twenty, better than Pa expected."

"That's good," Ernest said. "Well—what do you want to do?"

"I'd better get back early," Vera said. "Let's go sit on our hill."

Ernest drove the two miles west and parked on top of the hill. He pulled a blanket from the backseat and they huddled together, looking through the windshield. Vera wished they had a bed, tonight of all nights, but at twenty she already knew that holding a man with her body was no guarantee of lasting affection. There had to be more added as she groped her way past thirty toward forty, and began the long walk into fifty, sixty, and whatever lay beyond. But how could she learn, where could she go to learn, what were those bits and pieces? At ten o'clock she said, "I'd better get some sleep," and Ernest drove her home, walked her to the door, and kissed her goodnight.

"Tomorrow night?"

"Ma and Freda are driving into Slayton tomorrow afternoon. They want me to go along and we might not get home until late. Let's wait."

"All right."

"You won't be mad?"

"Tomorrow's my Sunday to work anyway."

Vera kissed him again. "They'll be going home Tuesday or Wednesday. I'll let you know."

"Fine."

"One more for the road." Vera kissed him so hard and long that both were breathless when she broke away and opened the door. Ernest saw her outlined against the light, hands stretching toward him as she closed the door.

EVERYTHING WAS READY by suppertime Sunday night. Vera helped her mother set the table for five, with two plates on the buffet for Les and Nels, in case somebody drove into the yard and they had to duck out of sight. After supper, when the dishes were done and they joined the men around the dining room table for their last review session, Vera slipped into her mackinaw, wrapped a muffler around her neck, and put on her stocking cap and mittens.

"Going for a walk," she called. "Be back soon."

She had no clear destination or reason for braving the night, but she crossed the yard into the barn and went out the far end past the machine shed where the getaway car was hidden under the big tarp. She stopped at the windmill and felt the steel-cold chill of the water tank rim penetrate the palm of her mitten; windmill and water tank were pumped full of childhood memories. She walked through her own spent time toward tomorrow's realization of all dreams, thinking of her first dream that had never come true and feeling the last dream that was fairly within her grasp. She wanted so much from life and she was not afraid to pay the price when she considered what she might become if only she could channel all her energy and passion in the right direction. She walked in open-eyed blindness until cold pinched her cheeks and turned her toward the house. She found everyone grouped around Les, sitting on a chair with his left foot in a tub of water. She said, "What happened?" and Les glared at her, speechless with rage at himself. Lucille said, "He tripped."

"Where?"

"Going down the back porch steps in the dark," Gus said.

"Going out to take a leak, with a bathroom in the house!"

Vera knelt and looked at the foot. Les's left foot was his clutch foot; tomorrow he had to be able to shift the V-8 gears as swiftly and smoothly as expert ability permitted him to double-clutch from first through second into high, and down again whenever necessary. He could not shift cleanly if the pain was so intense it made him flinch every time his left foot struck the clutch pedal. Vera looked up.

"Can you drive tomorrow?"

Les groaned. "I doubt it!"

Vera looked at their faces. No one spoke of cancelling. They wanted the money so badly that nothing else mattered. But they had to have a driver. She said, "You need three in the bank."

Gus nodded curtly.

"Who drives?"

They choked on their words, but Les swallowed his pain and spoke furiously, "There's a better driver than me right here!"

Twelve

A FEW MINUTES before four o'clock on Monday afternoon, Lionel Maas went to the implement shop office to check a part number for the tractor he and Shorty LaFollette were overhauling. Standing behind the counter, opening the bulky parts catalog, he glanced through the plate glass window and saw a dark blue 1935 V-8 sedan appear in his frame of view from the south and stop parallel to the curb in front of the bank. Three men got out and walked swiftly into the bank; through the bank windows, Lionel saw guns come up and watched Emma's arms jerk above her head like a puppet on strings. As Bob Conklin backed from his desk toward the rear wall, Lionel's instincts worked faster than his unbelieving eyes. He lifted the telephone and rang central.

"Number, please?"

"They're robbing the bank!"

Stella gasped as she plugged into the gas station and the lumberyard lines: "They're robbing the bank, go ahead, Lionel!"

A FEW MINUTES before four o'clock, Ernest crossed the street to the lumberyard and stood at the high desk, talking with Pete Olson. Pat Brown and Patrick had driven to Bent Fork but promised to return in time for Patrick and Ernest to pick up Lionel and get in an hour's hunting east of Lang's. Ernest had started toward the front door when the telephone rang and Pete Olson stepped into the office and lifted the receiver.

"Lumberyard . . . he's right here"—Pete raised his voice— "Ernest, they're robbing the bank!"

Ernest changed direction in mid-stride, swung around the end of the glass-fronted showcase, opened the gun cabinet and lifted Patrick's rifle from its niche in the corner. Pete called, "Ernest, where's Franklin, he don't answer the phone."

"Delivering gas."

"Delivering gas," Pete spoke into his telephone. "Ernest's going to use Patrick's gun."

As Ernest eased the rifle out, he pocketed half a dozen loose cartridges from the open box and was moving toward the front door, pumping a cartridge from the loaded magazine into the chamber, when Pete relayed Lionel's first words.

"They're behind the counter!"

Ernest opened the front door and swung it all the way back against the corner of the window showcase.

"They're at the floor safe and the vault!"

Ernest took his position on the left side of the doorway and brought the rifle up and tracked the route the car must follow, from the right-hand door casing to the left-hand casing.

"It's a 1935 dark blue V-8 sedan!"

Ernest brushed the front and rear sights with the ball of his right thumb. It was so long since they had sighted the rifles and worked out their firing positions that he had nearly forgotten the possibility of the bank being robbed.

STANDING AGAINST THE rear wall, Bob Conklin watched the robbery. One man went to the vault, another opened the floor safe, while the third stood at the corner of Bob's desk, watching everything inside the bank from the front door to the rear. When the other two finished cleaning out the vault and the floor safe, he motioned them toward Emma's window. They opened her cash drawer, scooped out the paper money, and moved along the ledge toward the second teller window. The tall man said, "Skip it!" and waved them past the drawer. They hurried through the swinging gate and waited for him at the front door, and Bob Conklin was suddenly aware that no one had bothered to open the second cash drawer. By God, he thought, they know we don't use it. They must be local! He looked more closely at them, trying to detect some clue to their identity behind their papier-mâché masks and ordinary clothing. The tall man sidled through the swinging gate, watching Bob Conklin and Emma as he backed toward the front door. His eyes through the shadowed holes in the mask met Bob Conklin's intent gaze. He realized his mistake at the same moment Bob Conklin seemed to guess some dead giveaway. He raised his heavy revolver and fired one shot that slammed Bob Conklin against the wall. Emma screamed and dropped on her knees beside Bob, and the tall man said, "Get out!" and they fled.

LIONEL SAID, "THEY shot Bob!"

"They shot Bob!" Pete Olson called.

Stella asked, "Lionel, can you tell how badly?"

"No," Lionel said, "but he's down and they're coming out!"

"They're coming out!" Pete Olson called.

Ernest shoved a sixth cartridge from his jacket pocket into the magazine. If he had any doubts, he lost all. Pat Brown had spoken the truth: No one had the right to come into their town, their bank, and rob, shoot, and kill. Ernest moved the rifle to the high ready.

"No hostage," Lionel said. "They're getting into the car!"

Stella plugged in Bent Fork's central: "This is Cherrygrove emergency. Give me Doctor Black's office."

"No hostage," Pete Olson called. "They're getting into the car."

Stella plugged in Blackbird central: "This is Cherrygrove emergency. Give me the sheriff's office."

"They're pulling out," Lionel said. "Going north toward the highway!"

Lionel heard Shorty LaFollette come from the shop, pat his shoulder to signify that all was understood, and duck into the supply room to get their shotguns.

"Coming north!" Pete called.

It had been planned that Patrick would be at the lumberyard doorway and Ernest would be across the street in the gas station doorway. As it had been agreed and practiced, Patrick would start shooting at the rear end of the getaway car while Ernest took the front end. But Patrick was gone and Franklin Krug was delivering gas and Ernest stood on the west side of Main Street in Patrick's position. Ernest brought the rifle to his shoulder and snugged it close, set his cheek comfortably, and sighted past the vertical line of the right-hand door casing. He began counting seconds in his head, waiting for the dark blue V-8 sedan to appear in his eye's sight. He had to start with the left front tire and work back, and if that did not stop the car, it made no difference that he did not want to kill anyone, he had to stop them, and the only way he could do that was to stop the driver.

The blue V-8 came into sight. Ernest shot the left front tire and pumped, shot into the engine and pumped, shot the left rear tire and pumped. The car lurched to the right but kept on, leaping with the uneven action of the blown tires as the driver pressed the footfeed and held speed, and even then, as an arm thrust from the left rear-door window and began firing a heavy revolver in the general direction of the lumberyard, Ernest aimed past the driver's hat to break the windshield and ruin vision. As he squeezed the trigger, the left front tire jumped and caused the driver's head to move forward. The car slowed and the front wheels veered to the right; the car ran off the street up the ramp leading into the elevator, dropped a right front wheel off the right side of the ramp and high-centered on the concrete retaining wall, came to a shuddering halt and slid backward a few feet to a dead stop. Ernest took four cartridges from his jacket pocket and reloaded as he stepped through the doorway, crossed the scale platform, and walked cattycorner across the street toward the car, rifle at the high post, cocked, finger on the trigger, watching the movement inside.

The arm holding the revolver in the left rear-door window suddenly crooked and raised the revolver toward the sky, then dropped it and fumbled for the door handle. On the right side, both doors opened and the two men in those seats threw their guns out and away, and stepped from the car, arms up. The hand fumbling for the left rear-door handle made contact, opened the door, and dropped limply to the side of the tall man who got out and stood slump-shouldered, staring across the street at Ernest, papier-mâché mask a woebegone shadow hiding the ghost of whatever it was he had lost.

In his field of vision, Ernest caught movement to his far right and heard Lionel call, "Patrick's back!" and down the street he saw the Nash turn off the highway, cross the bridge, and slide to a stop two car lengths from the railroad tracks. Patrick was out the passenger's side with his shotgun, Pat Brown was out and standing behind his door, shotgun barrel on the windowsill, backing up Patrick. Pete Olson spoke behind Ernest, "Right behind you!" and raised his voice, "You there! Keep your arms up, get away from that car!" Ernest walked toward the left front door and looked down through the open window at the driver. The force of his shot had slammed the driver's head forward, knocked the old felt hat off, and fanned the golden-brown hair across the steering wheel.

PATRICK REACHED ERNEST'S side just before Ernest looked into the car, and Lionel arrived a split second later. Patrick took one look and cradled his shotgun, reached over and took the rifle from Ernest's hands, lowered the trigger, and took Ernest's left arm as Lionel took his right. Pat Brown came up behind them, looked into the car, and said, "Take Ernest home!" in a tone Patrick had never heard before. They walked Ernest around the gas station up the street to his house, while sound grew behind them as people came running to help and, in horror, understood.

Doctor Black drove from Bent Fork in less than fifteen minutes. He went straight to the bank, took care of Bob Conklin, and came to Stonecifer's, where Ernest sat in a parlor rocker with Patrick and Lionel on either side. Doctor Black said, "Hello, Ernest," and Ernest answered in his usual calm, quiet voice, "Hello, Doc," but it was not his voice, nor was the face his face. Doctor Black said, "Let's get Ernest into bed, hmm?" and they led him across the hall and sat him on the edge of his bed. Doctor Black placed his bag on the dresser, opened it, and spoke while he reached inside.

"Get Ernest ready for bed."

Mrs. Stonecifer took a clean pair of pajamas from the top dresser drawer. They changed Ernest and eased him into bed, got him stretched out and apparently relaxed, head on the pillow, arms above the covers. Doctor Black made the injection and wiped the needle.

"Just let go, Ernest. You'll be asleep in a minute."

Ernest said, "All right, Doc," and closed his eyes. They watched him accept the morphine, but he shuddered once as some terrible thought raced through his mind. Then he slept.

"Don't leave him alone for a minute," Doctor Black said. "*Not one minute!* Not to go to the bathroom or anywhere else. Get all the medicine and razor blades out of the medicine cabinet right now. Mrs. Stonecifer, you can't do this yourself. I want two men with him all the time."

"Yes, sir," Patrick said.

"Doc," Lionel said, "how is Bob Conklin?"

"Thank God for lousy shots!" Doctor Black said. "The bullet got him high in the right shoulder and went straight through. A nice clean wound. I've got him bandaged and comfortable at home. I'm going over now for a second look, and I'll be back in the morning."

Doctor Black picked up his bag, tipped the hat he had not removed, and hurried out. Patrick said, "We'll stay, Mrs. Stonecifer."

Ernest's mother nodded in gratitude. "I'll get another chair."

Waiting, Patrick asked, "Which one shot Bob?"

Unwilling to speak the name, Lionel said, "The tall one."
They both knew that Gus Stensrud had been rated an expert
marksman during the war, known as a dead shot with the army
.45-caliber automatic. Doctor Black had said "Thank God for
lousy shots!" but was it?

They sat with Ernest until Jim Lang and Pat Brown relieved
them at midnight. They next day a regular schedule was worked
out: Patrick and Lionel sat with Ernest from eight in the morning
until four in the afternoon. Pete Olson and Shorty LaFollette took
over from four until midnight, and Jim and Ruth Lang from midnight until eight in the morning. On the nights Lionel drove livestock to market and had to get some sleep the next morning,
Walter Kelton came in from the farm, and others volunteered,
more than were needed.

They took Ernest to Bent Fork on the tenth day and Doctor
Black gave him a thorough physical examination that, Patrick
knew, was a coverup for the real purpose of trying to detect any
telltale signs that Ernest was so despondent he might try to take
his own life. Patrick could have told Doctor Black that Ernest
would not do that. Oh, in the beginning, anything might have
happened under such terrible pressure, but not now. Ernest was
looking at them again, and most important, looking at himself,
feeling himself. Doctor Black told Pat Brown and Patrick that it
would take a long time before Ernest fully recovered, but he had
every confidence that Ernest would. Ernest was too strong and
too honest with himself to let everything go to pieces and blame
it on an act over which he had had absolute control and thus, in
a strange and paradoxical way, no control at all.

"You understand, Patrick?"

"Yes, sir."

"Do you think Ernest ought to make a change?"

"Go away?"

"Yes."

"That's up to him, Doctor."

"Could he go with you?"

"Of course he can," Pat Brown said, "if he wants to."

"That's what I told him," Doctor Black said. "He thanked me and said it was nice of all of us to suggest it, but he'd rather stay at home."

That was Ernest, Patrick thought proudly. He had never run from anything in his life and he was not going to start now.

Thirteen

NOR DID HE. The last cold, gray days of October were gone, and it was time for Patrick to go. On the last night, Ernest and Lionel and Patrick met at the gas station and walked north across the highway, up the slope, to the corner of the dance pavilion, where they looked beyond the bare infield dirt and brown outfield grass at the horizon and the diamond-hard stars in a black sky. They turned without speaking and retraced their steps down the slope, across the highway and the bridge, over the railroad tracks to the lumberyard office porch. They stood where they had lived, in the town lying among the bare trees within the circle of worn hills beneath the slate sky, the little town turned grayer through the years since its heyday as a charter member of railroad aristocracy; it had sparkled briefly anew during the war and into the twenties with the false hopes and dreams of the era, then subsided into the dimness of the thirties that obscured shape and destroyed vitality until few people remembered that early spirit or seemed to care why the town was born and what it stood for. Patrick said, "Take care of yourselves," and they knew what he really meant. He was telling Lionel to watch over Ernest, and he was telling Ernest to stay alive until the pain of death was worse in his mind than the agony of living in his heart.

Night wind rattled the leaves in the ditch, blew wisps of dust through passing headlight beams. They tried to irradiate the past, but what was past? A few images blown into momentary light, dear faces, silent laughter, dried tears, the seasons that began in the springtime of a child's life and marched into his moment of departure.

Fiction Or6e
12/98
O'Rourke, Frank, 1916-

Ellen and the barber :

ALBANY COUNTY
PUBLIC LIBRARY
LARAMIE, WYOMING

DEMCO